THE BOOK OF

SLOW COOKING

THE BOOK OF

SLOW
COOKING

ANNE SHEASBY

PHOTOGRAPHED BY
PATRICK McLEAVEY

HPBooks

ANOTHER BEST SELLING VOLUME FROM HPBOOKS

HPBooks
Published by the Berkley Publishing Group
A division of Penguin Putnam Inc.
375 Hudson Street
New York, NY 10014

Copyright © 2003 by Salamander Books Ltd.
By arrangement with Salamander Books Ltd.

A member of **Chrysalis** Books plc

Project managed by: Stella Caldwell
Editor: Madeline Weston
Photographer: Patrick McLeavey
Designer: Sue Storey
Home Economist: Sandra Miles
Production: Don Campaniello
Filmset and reproduction by: Studio Tec, England

First edition: February 2003

Visit our website at www.penguinputnam.com

This book has been cataloged with the Library of Congress

ISBN 1-55788-404-8

Printed and bound in Spain

10 9 8 7 6 5 4 3 2 1

CONTENTS

INTRODUCTION 6

SOUPS & STARTERS 12

MEAT & FISH DISHES 26

POULTRY & GAME DISHES 42

VEGETARIAN & VEGETABLE DISHES 56

PUDDINGS & DESSERTS 68

CAKES & TEABREADS 80

CHUTNEYS & PRESERVES 87

HOT PUNCHES & BEVERAGES 92

INDEX 96

INTRODUCTION

Slow cookers have been around for many years and are often forgotten or lost in the back of a cupboard. However, in recent years, they have been making a great comeback and you'll be both surprised and delighted at how versatile they really can be.

Slow cookers can be used day or night, are simple and economical to use, and require little or no attention once you have initially prepared the ingredients. It is hard to beat the aroma of a delicious casserole, soup or hotpot, perfectly cooked and ready to eat, when you walk through the door at the end of a busy, tiring day. You don't need to worry that the pot may burn dry or that you are using up too much energy and you can save on doing the dishes too!

Slow cooking has come on by leaps and bounds in the last few years and now you are able to prepare any number of delicious recipes in a slow cooker, including tasty soups, pâtés, fondue, casseroles, curries, and risotto. Slow-cooked desserts such as fruit compote, crème caramel, and bread and butter pudding are a real treat, and even tempting cakes and sweet treats such as teabreads and sponge cakes can be successfully cooked in a slow cooker. Chutneys, preserves, and hot fruit punches add another inviting dimension to the world of slow cooking.

As foods are cooked slowly, usually for long periods of time, meat and vegetables become deliciously tender (and this applies to even the cheapest, toughest cuts of meat) and slow cooking retains all the goodness and enhances and develops the color and flavor of the foods. There is less evaporation so there is little chance of the food drying out.

If you enjoy good home-cooked food but have little time to spend cooking, introduce yourself to slow cooking and you'll be pleasantly surprised and pleased with how easy and versatile this fuss-free, modern-day method of cooking really is. So, now its time to dig out your slow cooker and shake off the dust, or treat yourself to a new one and get slow cooking!

At the end of each recipe in this book, we give some serving suggestion ideas, as well as the quantity or number of servings each recipe makes. Some recipes also include additional ideas for ingredient variations to change the flavor of the basic recipe to suit your own tastes, as well as the occasional Cook's Tip.

CHOOSING A SLOW COOKER

There is a good selection of slow cookers in a range of sizes, shape,s and colors to suit your requirements and many are widely available at a modest price. They vary in capacity, from approximately 7 cups to 5 or 6 quarts, but all slow cookers operate at a low wattage and consume a similar amount of electricity. Also, the efficient insulation built into the slow cooker ensures that only the food inside the cooker heats up and not the whole kitchen. Buying a slow cooker with a larger capacity enables you to cook a much wider range of dishes and cater for more people. Settings vary but choose a slow cooker that meets all your needs.

REMOVABLE-POT SLOW COOKERS

The most common slow cookers have a removable inner earthenware or ceramic cooking pot. The outer casing of these models may be made of metal such as aluminum, or heat resistant plastic, and is fitted with an inner metal casing. The removable cooking pot sits in the inner casing and the heating elements are situated between the inner and outer casings.

This type of slow cooker enables you to take the cooking pot to the table for serving, rather than moving the whole slow cooker. It also usually means that food can be browned or crisped under the broiler without the risk of damaging the outer casing of the slow cooker. Lids are made of heat-resistant glass or ceramic.

FIXED-POT SLOW COOKERS

Other less common slow cookers comprise an earthenware or ceramic pot that is permanently fixed into an outer casing and incorporates heating elements between the outer casing and the cooking pot. Some slow cookers also have a detachable electric cable.

Slow cookers with removable cooking pots are more versatile.

GUIDELINES WHEN FIRST USING YOUR SLOW COOKER

It is always very important to read through the manufacturer's instructions before using your slow cooker for the first time. Each slow cooker model will vary slightly and even on the same setting, some will cook faster or slower than others. Because of this, it is a good idea to use your slow cooker several times and get used to it, before trying any of the recipes in this book. That way you will know exactly how your slow cooker works and cooks different foods.

The timings given in the recipes in this book are an accurate guide, but you may find that your slow cooker cooks more quickly or more slowly, so, if necessary, simply adjust the cooking times accordingly.

CONTROLS / SETTINGS

Controls on slow cookers vary slightly but most have three basic settings – OFF, LOW and HIGH – others also include an AUTO setting. Most models have a power indicator light which lights up and remains on when the slow cooker is in operation. On the LOW setting, the slow cooker will cook foods very gently with hardly any simmering. On the HIGH setting, the cooker will cook at its highest power and may simmer and actually boil some foods and liquids. With the AUTO setting, cooking starts at a high temperature, then automatically switches to a LOW cook. The temperature is thermostatically controlled and, in some cases, the indicator light may cycle on and off during cooking. With other models on the AUTO setting, the light remains on constantly during cooking. Most of the recipes in this book use the HIGH or LOW settings.

PREHEATING SLOW COOKERS

Before starting many recipes (always refer to manufacturer's instructions for your specific model), the slow cooker may need to be preheated on HIGH for about 20 minutes. This preheating time can often be the time that you spend preparing the ingredients. To preheat your slow cooker (if applicable) simply place the empty cooking pot in the slow cooker base, place the lid in position, plug in and switch on with the control set on HIGH. Once the cooker is preheated, add the prepared ingredients to the cooking pot, replace the lid, and continue cooking as directed in the recipe.

CARING FOR & CLEANING YOUR SLOW COOKER

Refer to the manufacturer's guidelines about caring for your slow cooker. Before using a slow cooker for the first time, ensure that you wash it in warm, soapy water and rinse and dry it thoroughly. After each use, remove and empty the cooking pot, switch the slow cooker off, and fill the cooking pot with warm water, leave to soak for a few minutes, if necessary, then wash, rinse and dry as before.

Do not subject the cooking pot to sudden changes in temperature and never plunge it into cold or boiling water. Do not leave the cooking pot immersed in water as this may adversely effect the porous base. Remove any stubborn stains with a soft brush or nylon cleaning pad. Do not use abrasive cleaners or scourers on the cooking pot or outer casing of your slow cooker.

The outer casing of the slow cooker should never be immersed in water, filled with water, or used for cooking without the inner cooking pot. Food or liquid should never be put into the metal inner lining of the outer casing. If the outer casing needs cleaning, wipe it clean with a cloth soaked in warm, soapy water.

The slow cooker lid should also be washed in warm, soapy water, rinsed and dried thoroughly. Most cooking pots and lids are not suitable for washing in a dishwasher, but it is worth checking with the instructions for your specific model. Many of the cooking pots or lids cannot be used in an oven, freezer, or microwave or on a conventional stove—again, check the specific manufacturer's instructions.

After cooking, always remember to use oven gloves to remove the cooking pot from the slow cooker base, as the pot will be hot. Use oven gloves also when removing the lid.

ADAPTING YOUR OWN RECIPES

When adapting your own recipes to cook in the slow cooker, simply refer to similar recipes in this book or in the manufacturer's handbook and adapt cooking times accordingly. This way you can add even more ideas to your growing repertoire of slow cooker recipes.

It is worth remembering that because there is less evaporation in a slow cooker, you should always reduce the quantity of liquid used when adapting recipes for this method of cooking. In a slow cooker, the steam condenses on the lid and returns to the pot and, in doing so, forms a seal around the lid that retains heat and flavor. As a useful guide, use about half the quantity of liquid given in the conventional recipe. You can always add a little more boiling liquid at the end of the cooking time if the result is too thick.

If you wish to reduce the quantity of liquid at the end of the cooking time, remove the lid after cooking, turn the setting to HIGH, and reduce by simmering for about 30-45 minutes.

TIPS FOR PREPARING FOOD AND INGREDIENTS

Trim excess fat from meat and cut meat into small, even, bite-size pieces. It is important to cut vegetables, especially root vegetables, into small dice, small, bite-size pieces, or thin slices as, surprisingly, they often take longer to cook than meat in a slow cooker. Place the diced vegetables in the base or towards the bottom half of the cooking pot and ensure that they are covered completely with liquid.

You can also speed up the cooking a little by precooking vegetables in oil or butter in a pan to soften before adding them to the slow cooker—this is known as the browning method and many of the recipes in this book use this method, where applicable. Pre-browning or sealing meat in oil or melted butter in a pan before adding it to the slow cooker, also improves the appearance, texture and flavor of the cooked dish. It is often a good idea to bring the cooking liquid to the boil before adding it to the slow cooker.

If you don't have time to precook meat or vegetables this is fine—this is known as the one-step method, but you will need to increase the recommended cooking time of the recipe, normally by about 2-3 hours.

If using the one-step method of cooking, preheat the slow cooker on HIGH while preparing the ingredients. Place the finely chopped vegetables in the base of the cooking pot, add the meat or poultry, then add the herbs or seasonings and pour over enough boiling stock or liquid to just cover the food. Switch the setting to LOW and cook as instructed—you will need to add about 2 or 3 hours to the minimum recommended cooking time for the recipe.

Food should be seasoned lightly with salt and pepper, especially salt.

Add the minimum amount of salt and then check and adjust the seasoning before serving.

Frozen ingredients should always be defrosted thoroughly before placing them in a slow cooker. Usually defrosted frozen vegetables are added towards the end of the cooking time.

Dried beans should be soaked in plenty of cold water for at least 10 hours or overnight. The beans should then be drained, placed in a large pan, covered with fresh cold water, and boiled for 10 minutes, then drained and used as required. Red kidney beans should be boiled rapidly for 10 minutes, to kill any toxins present. Lentils do not need precooking. Use quick-cooking varieties of rice and pasta.

As a general rule, to avoid separation or curdling, dairy products such as cream and milk are best added towards the end of the cooking time or at the end of cooking, if possible. Refer to individual recipes for guidance. It is best to use whole (full-fat / full-cream) milk, rather than semi-skimmed or skimmed milk, in recipes.

Thickening agents can be added at the beginning or towards the end of the cooking time. Flour should be added at the start; for example, once the meat and vegetables have been browned and softened, a little flour may be stirred in before the cooking liquid is added, brought to the boil and then transferred to the cooking pot.

Alternatively, cornstarch, blended with a little water, can be stirred into a dish for the last 30-60 minutes of the cooking time. You may need to use a little more thickener than in conventional recipes, as slow cooking can produce more liquid.

Use dried herbs rather than fresh. Dried herbs create a better flavour during the long, slow cooking, but to further enhance the flavour and appearance of dishes, chopped fresh herbs can be stirred into the finished dish or sprinkled on top.

USEFUL HINTS AND TIPS WHEN USING A SLOW COOKER

It is best to leave the slow cooker undisturbed during cooking and, unless the recipe specifies otherwise, do not lift the lid during the cooking process, as this will break the water seal around the rim and will interfere with the cooking time. With most recipes, there is no need to turn or stir the food, as it will not stick, burn, or bubble over, and slow cooking provides a very even method of cooking. If you do feel the need to lift the lid, you will need to increase the cooking time by about 20-30 minutes in order to allow the slow cooker to regain lost heat.

As an approximate guide, the cooking time on HIGH is just over half of that on LOW. If you need to speed the cooking process up, simply switch the control to the HIGH setting.

Dishes to be cooked in a slow cooker should always contain or use some liquid.

Do not store uncooked food or ingredients in the slow cooker, either at room temperature or in the fridge. If you are not going to cook the prepared foods immediately, store them in a separate container in the refrigerator until ready to use.

When cooking joints of meat or foods that are cooked in dishes such as pudding basins, ensure that the food or dish fits comfortably in the cooking pot and that the lid fits securely before cooking begins.

Ideally slow cookers should be filled to a maximum of ½-1 inch from the top of the cooking pot, but they should be at least half-full and no more than three-quarters full.

Once the cooking time is complete, food may be kept hot by switching the setting to LOW.

If, at the end of cooking time, the food is not ready, replace the lid, switch the setting to HIGH, and continue cooking for a further 30-60 minutes, or until the food is thoroughly cooked.

With dishes such as soups and casseroles, once the cooking time is complete, always stir the dish well before serving.

If required, a quick and easy way of blending / puréeing soups before serving, is to use a hand-held electric blender. Carefully blend the soup until it is of the desired consistency, taking care not to touch the cooking pot with the blender. The soup is then ready to serve. Otherwise, if required, the cooked soup should be cooled slightly, puréed in a blender or food processor until smooth, then reheated in a saucepan on the stove before serving.

Cakes cooked in a slow cooker do not brown in the way that they do when baked in a conventional oven, so they are often paler in color. Frosting spread on top of a cooked cake, or sugar or nuts sprinkled over the top of it, will improve its appearance. However, other cakes such as chocolate cake and gingerbread cooked in a slow cooker contain plenty of color just from their ingredients.

When cooking cakes and some desserts in the slow cooker, if the recipe calls for a cake tin, always use cake tins with fixed / non removable bases (rather than loose-based tins or springform tins).

When making cakes, if the recipe instructs the tin or dish to be greased and lined, try using one of the pre-shaped non-stick baking parchment liners now readily available. These liners come in various shapes and sizes from good cook shops and hardware stores. They simply fit into the tin with no need for greasing, so saving time and effort.

Any leftover cooked food should be removed from the slow cooker, cooled quickly, then chilled or frozen. Cold cooked food should not be reheated in the slow cooker as it will not reach a high enough temperature to be safe to eat.

A large-sized slow cooker makes an ideal companion to your freezer if you like to make extra quantities to freeze for a later date.

BACON & CORN CHOWDER

2 tablespoons butter
8oz smoked Canadian bacon slices, diced
1 large onion, chopped
3 stalks celery, finely chopped
3 cups finely diced potatoes
2¼ cups sliced button mushrooms
4 cups vegetable stock
salt and freshly ground black pepper
12oz can corn kernels, drained
4-6 tablespoons light cream
3-4 tablespoons chopped fresh parsley

Preheat the slow cooker on HIGH while preparing the ingredients.

Melt butter in a pan, add bacon and cook for 3 minutes, stirring. Add onion, celery, and potatoes and sauté for 5 minutes. Add mushrooms, stock, and seasoning and stir to mix. Bring to a boil, then transfer to the cooking pot. Cover, reduce the temperature to LOW, and cook for 6 hours.

Stir in corn, cover, and cook on LOW for a further 1-2 hours. Stir in cream and chopped parsley and adjust the seasoning to taste. Ladle into warmed soup bowls and serve with warm crusty bread or cornmeal bread.

Serves 4-6

VARIATION: Thicken the soup with a little cornstarch, if liked. Blend 1-2 tablespoons cornstarch with a little water and stir into the soup. Cook on HIGH for 20-30 minutes.

PEA & HAM SOUP

1 onion
2 leeks, washed
1lb fresh peas (shelled weight)
1 clove garlic, crushed (optional)
4½ cups vegetable stock
salt and freshly ground black pepper
2 cups diced, cooked, lean smoked ham
chopped fresh parsley, to garnish

Preheat the slow cooker on HIGH while preparing the ingredients. Finely chop onion and thinly slice leeks.

Place all the ingredients except ham and parsley in the cooking pot and stir to mix. Cover, reduce the temperature to LOW, and cook for 7-8 hours. Cool slightly, then purée the mixture in a blender or food processor until smooth.

Return the soup to the rinsed-out cooking pot and stir in ham. Cover and cook on LOW for 1-2 hours. Ladle into warmed soup bowls, garnish with chopped parsley, and serve with crusty French bread.

Serves 4-6

VARIATION: Use 2½ cups unsmoked ham in place of smoked ham, if preferred.

LEEK & POTATO SOUP

2 tablespoons butter
1 onion, finely chopped
1lb leeks (trimmed weight), washed and thinly sliced
4 cups finely diced potatoes
4 cups vegetable stock
salt and freshly ground black pepper
⅔ cup light or heavy cream
chopped fresh chives, to garnish

Preheat the slow cooker on HIGH while preparing the ingredients. Melt butter in a pan, add onion and leeks, and cook gently for 5 minutes, stirring occasionally.

Add potatoes and cook gently for 10 minutes, or until softened, stirring occasionally. Add stock and seasoning, then bring to a boil. Transfer to the cooking pot, cover, then reduce the temperature to LOW and cook for 7-9 hours.

Cool slightly, then purée the mixture in a blender or food processor until smooth. Return the soup to the rinsed-out cooking pot and stir in cream. Cover and cook on LOW for 30-60 minutes, or until hot. Ladle into warmed soup bowls, sprinkle with chopped chives, and serve with soft bread rolls.

Serves 4

VARIATION: Use milk in place of cream.

— PLUM TOMATO & BASIL SOUP —

2¼lb plum tomatoes
2 tablespoons olive oil, plus extra for croutons
1 large red onion, thinly sliced
2 cloves garlic, crushed
1 red bell pepper, seeded, and thinly sliced
2 tablespoons sun-dried tomato paste
2 teaspoons sugar
4 cups vegetable stock
salt and freshly ground black pepper
4 slices day-old mixed seed bread, crusts trimmed
4 tablespoons chopped fresh basil
fresh Parmesan cheese shavings, to serve

Preheat the slow cooker on HIGH while preparing the ingredients.

Using a sharp knife, cut a small cross in base of each tomato; place in a bowl, cover with boiling water, and leave for 30 seconds. Remove and plunge into cold water; drain. Peel, then chop flesh and set aside. Heat oil in a large pan, add onion, garlic, and red bell pepper and sauté for 5 minutes. Stir in tomatoes, tomato paste, sugar, stock, and seasoning, then bring to a boil. Transfer to the cooking pot, cover, switch setting to AUTO and cook for 6-8 hours (or LOW for 8-10 hours). Cool slightly, then purée in a blender or food processor until smooth.

Return soup to the rinsed-out cooking pot, cover, and cook on LOW for 30-60 minutes, or until hot. Meanwhile, make croutons. Cut bread into 1 inch squares. Heat a ¼ inch depth of oil in a skillet. Add bread cubes and fry, turning frequently, until crisp and golden. Remove and drain on paper towels. Stir chopped basil into the soup and serve in warmed soup bowls. Sprinkle croutons and Parmesan shavings over the top.

Serves 6

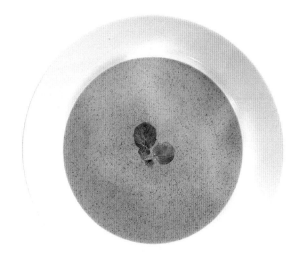

― CREAMY WATERCRESS SOUP ―

2 tablespoons butter
6 shallots, finely chopped
1 leek, washed and thinly sliced
2 cups diced potatoes
8oz watercress, roughly chopped
3⅓ cups vegetable stock
salt and freshly ground black pepper
⅔ cup light cream

Preheat the slow cooker on HIGH while preparing the ingredients. Melt butter in a pan, add shallots and leek, and sauté for 5 minutes.

Add potatoes and watercress and cook for 3 minutes or until the watercress wilts, stirring occasionally. Add the stock and seasoning, then bring to a boil. Transfer to the cooking pot, cover, then reduce the temperature to LOW and cook for 6-7 hours.

Cool slightly, then purée the mixture in a blender or food processor until smooth. Return the soup to the rinsed-out cooking pot and stir in cream. Cover and cook on LOW for 30-60 minutes, or until hot. Ladle into warmed soup bowls and serve with fresh bread rolls.

Serves 4

VARIATION: Use 1 onion in place of shallots.

— GARDEN VEGETABLE SOUP —

3 tablespoons butter
1 onion, thinly sliced
2 leeks, washed and thinly sliced
2 stalks celery, finely chopped
1½ cups thinly sliced carrots
1 cup diced parsnips
1½ cups diced potatoes
1 cup diced rutabaga
3 tablespoons all-purpose flour
4 cups vegetable stock
2 teaspoons dried herbes de Provence
salt and freshly ground black pepper
chopped fresh parsley, to garnish

Preheat the slow cooker on HIGH while preparing the ingredients. Melt butter in a large pan (see above). Add all the prepared vegetables and cook gently for 10 minutes or until softened, stirring occasionally. Stir in flour and cook for 1 minute, stirring. Gradually stir in stock, then add dried herbs and seasoning. Bring to a boil, stirring, then transfer to the slow cooker.

Cover, switch the setting to AUTO and cook for 6-8 hours (or LOW for 8-10 hours). Ladle into warmed soup bowls, sprinkle with chopped parsley, and serve with warm soda bread or wheaten bread.

Serves 4-6

VARIATIONS: Use turnip in place of rutabaga. Use sweet potatoes in place of standard potatoes.

FRESH MUSHROOM SOUP

½oz dried porcini mushrooms
2 tablespoons butter
1 onion, finely chopped
4½ cups thinly sliced mushrooms
3⅓ cups vegetable stock
salt and freshly ground black pepper
⅔ cup light cream
2 tablespoons chopped fresh flat-leaf parsley

Preheat the slow cooker on HIGH while preparing the ingredients. Place dried mushrooms in a small bowl, pour ½ cup boiling water over and leave to soak for 20 minutes.

Drain soaked mushrooms, reserving soaking liquid, then snip soaked mushrooms into small pieces using scissors. Set aside. Melt butter in a pan, add onion, and sauté for 3 minutes. Add fresh mushrooms and soaked dried mushrooms and cook gently for 5 minutes, stirring occasionally. Stir in stock, reserved mushroom liquid and seasoning, then bring to a boil. Transfer to the cooking pot, cover, reduce the temperature to LOW, and cook for 5 hours.

Stir in cream, cover, and cook on LOW for a further 30-60 minutes, or until hot. Alternatively, cool the soup slightly, purée in a blender or food processor until smooth, then return to the rinsed-out cooking pot. Stir in cream, cover, and cook on LOW for 30-60 minutes or until hot. Stir in chopped parsley and serve with warm Italian bread.

Serves 4

SPICY SQUASH SOUP

2 butternut squash (about 2½lb total weight)
2 tablespoons butter
2 onions, thinly sliced
2 stalks celery, finely chopped
1 clove garlic, crushed
1 teaspoon ground cumin
1 teaspoon ground coriander
1 teaspoon hot chili powder
3¾ cups vegetable stock
salt and freshly ground black pepper
⅔ cup light cream
4 slices smoked Canadian bacon
2 tablespoons chopped fresh cilantro

Preheat the slow cooker on HIGH while preparing the ingredients.

Remove and discard skin and seeds from squash, and finely chop flesh. Set aside (see above). Melt butter in a large pan, add onions, celery, and garlic and sauté for 5 minutes. Add squash and ground spices, and cook gently for 5 minutes, stirring occasionally. Add stock and seasoning, bring to a boil, then transfer to the cooking pot. Cover, reduce the temperature to LOW, and cook for 6-8 hours. Cool slightly, then purée mixture in a blender or food processor until smooth. Return soup to rinsed-out cooking pot and stir in cream.

Cover and cook on LOW for 30-60 minutes, or until hot. Meanwhile, make bacon croutons. Preheat broiler to high. Broil bacon until crisp all over, turning once. Drain on paper towels and set aside. Stir chopped cilantro into soup, then ladle into warmed soup bowls. Crumble bacon and sprinkle over the soup. Serve with warm crusty bread.

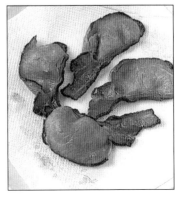

Serves 4

VARIATION: Use peeled and seeded pumpkin flesh in place of squash.

— THAI SPICED CHICKEN SOUP —

2 tablespoons sunflower oil
6 shallots, finely chopped
3 cups thinly sliced carrots
4 stalks celery, thinly sliced
1 clove garlic, crushed
1 red chili, seeded and finely chopped
1 inch piece fresh ginger root, peeled and
  finely chopped
1lb 2oz skinless, boneless chicken thighs, diced
1 tablespoon Thai seven-spice seasoning
¾ cup sliced green beans
4 cups chicken stock
salt and freshly ground black pepper
3oz spaghetti, broken into small lengths
2-3 tablespoons chopped fresh cilantro

Preheat the slow cooker on HIGH while preparing the ingredients. Heat oil in a pan, add shallots, carrots, celery, garlic, chili and ginger and sauté for 3 minutes (see above). Add chicken and cook until sealed all over, stirring frequently. Add Thai spice and green beans and cook for 1 minute, stirring. Add stock and seasoning and bring to a boil.

Transfer to the cooking pot, cover, then reduce the heat to LOW and cook for 5 hours. Stir in spaghetti, cover, and cook on LOW for a further 1-2 hours or until spaghetti is cooked and tender. Stir in chopped cilantro and serve with fresh crusty bread.

Serves 4-6

MEXICAN BEAN SOUP

1¼ cups dried red kidney beans
2 tablespoons olive oil
2 red onions, finely chopped
2 cloves garlic, crushed
1 red bell pepper, seeded and diced
1 fresh red chili, seeded and finely chopped
2 teaspoons ground coriander
1 teaspoon ground cumin
1¾ cups canned chopped tomatoes
3¾ cups vegetable stock
3 teaspoons chili sauce, plus extra to taste
salt and freshly ground black pepper
2-3 tablespoons chopped fresh cilantro
4 tablespoons heavy cream (optional)

Place kidney beans in a large bowl. Cover with plenty of cold water. Soak for at least 10 hours or overnight (see above). Preheat the slow cooker on HIGH while preparing the ingredients. Drain beans, place in a large pan, cover with cold water, and bring to a boil. Boil rapidly for 10 minutes, then rinse, drain, and set aside. Meanwhile, heat oil in a large pan, add onions, garlic, bell pepper, and chili and sauté for 5 minutes. Add ground spices and cook gently for 1 minute, stirring. Add kidney beans, tomatoes, stock, chili sauce, and seasoning and bring to a boil.

Transfer to the cooking pot, cover, reduce the temperature to LOW, and cook for 8-12 hours. Stir in the chopped cilantro and extra chili sauce, if liked. Stir in the heavy cream, if using, and ladle into warmed soup bowls. Serve with warm fresh bread.

Serves 4-6

CHEESE FONDUE

1 clove garlic, peeled and halved
2 cups coarsely grated Gruyère cheese
2 cups coarsely grated Emmental cheese
1 tablespoon cornstarch
1 tablespoon kirsch
scant 1 cup dry white wine
pinch of freshly grated nutmeg
freshly ground black pepper
chopped fresh parsley, to garnish

Rub the inside of the cooking pot of the slow cooker with cut side of garlic. Place Gruyère and Emmental cheeses in the cooking pot.

Blend cornstarch with kirsch in a small bowl and add to cheeses with wine and seasonings. Stir to mix well. Cover and cook on LOW for 3-4 hours, stirring occasionally, until the ingredients are melted and blended together and the fondue is hot.

Sprinkle with chopped parsley and serve with small chunks of crusty bread, vegetable crudités, and apple and pear slices.

Serves 4

VARIATION: Use beer or light ale in place of wine.

FARMHOUSE PÂTÉ

6 thin slices prosciutto
2 tablespoons butter
1 onion, finely chopped
1 clove garlic, crushed
1½ cups chopped mushrooms
8oz chicken livers, trimmed and diced
8oz skinless boneless chicken breast, diced
8oz ground pork
4oz bacon, diced
2 tablespoons brandy
2 tablespoons green peppercorns in brine, drained
4 teaspoons chopped fresh thyme
salt and freshly ground black pepper
herb sprigs, to garnish

Line base and sides of a 5 cup round ovenproof dish with prosciutto, allowing edges to hang over sides. Set aside (see above). Melt butter in a pan, add onion, garlic, and mushrooms and sauté for 5 minutes. Add chicken livers, chicken breast, ground pork, and bacon and cook until meat is colored all over, stirring frequently. Cool slightly, then process in a blender or food processor with the brandy. Transfer to a bowl and stir in peppercorns, chopped thyme, and seasoning. Mix well. Spoon into prepared dish and press down lightly.

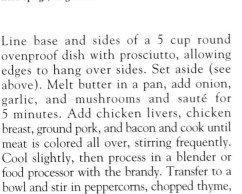

Fold prosciutto over pâté, then cover with foil. Place in the cooking pot and add sufficient boiling water to the cooking pot to come halfway up the sides of the dish. Cover and cook on HIGH for 5-6 hours or until cooked and the juices of the pâté run clear when pierced with a skewer. Lift out, remove the foil, drain off any excess juices, and leave to cool. Chill before serving. Turn out on to a serving plate and garnish with herb sprigs. Serve with crusty French bread.

Serves 8-10

CHICKEN LIVER PÂTÉ

6 slices rindless bacon
3 tablespoons butter
1 onion, finely chopped
2 cloves garlic, crushed
1lb chicken livers, trimmed and halved
2 tablespoons ruby port
2 tablespoons heavy cream
1½ teaspoons dried mixed herbs
salt and freshly ground black pepper
mixed salad leaves, to garnish

Stretch the bacon slices using the back of a knife. Line the base and sides of a 6 inch round ovenproof dish with the bacon. Set aside.

Melt butter in a pan, add onion and garlic, and cook gently for 5 minutes, stirring occasionally. Add chicken livers and cook for about 5 minutes or until sealed all over, stirring occasionally. Remove pan from the heat, cool slightly, then stir in port, cream, dried herbs, and seasoning. Purée mixture in a blender or food processor until smooth. Spoon into the prepared dish and level the surface.

Cover with foil. Place in the cooking pot of the slow cooker. Add sufficient boiling water to the cooking pot to come halfway up the sides of the dish. Cover and cook on HIGH for 5-6 hours or until thoroughly cooked. Lift out, remove the foil, and leave to cool. Chill before serving. Turn out on to a serving plate and garnish with salad leaves. Serve with toast or warm crusty bread.

Serves 6-8

EGGPLANT DIP

2lb eggplants
4 tablespoons olive oil
6 shallots, finely chopped
2 cloves garlic, crushed
8oz portobello mushrooms, chopped
1½ teaspoons ground coriander
1½ teaspoons ground cumin
4 tablespoons dry white wine
salt and freshly ground black pepper
4 tablespoons chopped fresh cilantro

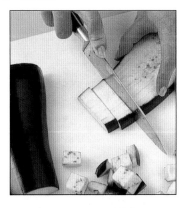

Trim and dice eggplants. Set aside. Heat oil in a large pan, add shallots and garlic, and sauté for 3 minutes.

Add eggplants and mushrooms and cook for 10-15 minutes or until soft, stirring occasionally. Add ground spices and cook for 1 minute, stirring. Remove the pan from the heat and cool slightly. Place the mixture in a blender or food processor with wine and seasoning and blend until smooth and well mixed.

Transfer the mixture to the cooking pot in the slow cooker and level the surface. Cover and cook on LOW for 4-5 hours. Stir in chopped cilantro, then serve warm, or cool and chill before serving. Serve with breadsticks, vegetable crudités, or toasted Italian bread.

Serves 6-8

VARIATION: If serving cold, stir 4-6 tablespoons heavy cream into the eggplant dip just before serving, if liked.

— BEEF GOULASH WITH CHILI —

2 tablespoons olive oil
1½lb lean round steak, cut into small dice
1 onion, sliced
1 clove garlic, crushed
4 cups peeled and finely diced potatoes
2 green bell peppers, seeded and thinly sliced
1 fresh green chili, seeded and thinly sliced
2 tablespoons all-purpose flour
1 tablespoon paprika
1¼ cups beef stock
1¾ cups canned chopped tomatoes
2 tablespoons tomato paste
pinch of caraway seeds
2 bay leaves
salt and freshly ground black pepper

Preheat the slow cooker on HIGH while preparing the ingredients. Heat oil in a pan, add beef, and cook until meat is sealed all over, stirring occasionally (see above). Transfer to the cooking pot using a slotted spoon. Set aside. Add onion, garlic, potatoes, bell peppers, and chili to the pan, and sauté for about 5 minutes, or until slightly softened. Stir in flour and paprika and cook for 1 minute, stirring. Gradually stir in stock, then add tomatoes, tomato paste, caraway seeds, bay leaves, and seasoning and mix well.

Bring to a boil, stirring, then transfer to the cooking pot and stir to mix. Cover, reduce, the temperature to LOW and cook for 10-12 hours, or until beef is cooked and tender. Remove and discard bay leaves and adjust seasoning. Serve with fresh bread or cooked noodles or rice.

Serves 4

—— TASTY BEEF & BEAN STEW ——

1¼ cups navy beans
3 tablespoons sunflower oil
1 large red onion, chopped
2 cloves garlic, crushed
2 red bell peppers, seeded and chopped
2 fresh red chilies, seeded and finely chopped
2lb lean round steak, cut into small dice
3 tablespoons all-purpose flour
3 teaspoons ground coriander
3 teaspoons ground cumin
salt and freshly ground black pepper
2 cups beef stock
⅔ cup red wine

Place beans in a large bowl. Cover with plenty of cold water and leave to soak for at least 10 hours or overnight (see above). Preheat the slow cooker on HIGH while preparing the ingredients. Drain beans, place in a large pan, cover with cold water, and bring to a boil. Boil for 10 minutes, then rinse, drain, and set aside. Meanwhile, heat 1 tablespoon oil in a large pan, add onion, garlic, bell peppers, and chilies and sauté for 5 minutes. Transfer to the cooking pot and set aside.

Toss the meat in the flour, ground spices, and seasoning until coated. Heat remaining oil in the pan, add meat in batches, and cook quickly until sealed. Transfer to the cooking pot. Add beans, stock, and wine to the pan and bring to a boil, stirring, scraping up any browned bits in the pan. Add to the cooking pot and stir to mix well. Cover, reduce temperature to LOW, and cook for 7-9 hours, or until beef is cooked and tender. Serve with cooked egg noodles or rice and green beans.

Serves 4-6

BEEF IN RED WINE

3 tablespoons butter
8oz lean smoked bacon, diced
2¼lb lean round steak, diced
¼ cup all-purpose flour
1¼ cups red wine such as Burgundy
⅔ cup beef stock
2 tablespoons brandy
16 baby onions or shallots
8oz button mushrooms
2 thyme sprigs
salt and freshly ground black pepper
1 cup self-rising flour
1 teaspoon baking powder
2oz shredded beef suet or vegetable shortening
1 teaspoon dry mustard
2 tablespoons chopped fresh mixed herbs

Preheat the slow cooker on HIGH while preparing the ingredients. Melt butter in a large pan, add bacon, and cook for 3 minutes, stirring. Add beef and cook until sealed all over, stirring occasionally (see above). Stir in flour and cook for 2 minutes, stirring. Gradually stir in wine, stock, and brandy. Add onions or shallots, mushrooms, thyme sprigs, and seasoning and bring to a boil, stirring. Transfer to the cooking pot. Cover, reduce temperature to LOW, and cook for 8-10 hours, until beef is cooked and tender. Remove and discard thyme sprigs.

Sift flour and baking powder into a bowl, stir in suet, mustard, chopped herbs, and seasoning. Add enough cold water (about 4-5 tablespoons) to make a firm dough. Divide dough into 16 pieces and, with floured hands, roll each piece into a small ball. Put dough balls all around edge of cooking pot on top of casserole. Cover, increase temperature to HIGH, and cook for 40-60 minutes or until dumplings are cooked. Serve with vegetables such as broccoli and baby new potatoes.

Serves 4

CURRIED POT ROAST BEEF

2 teaspoons turmeric
2 teaspoons ground coriander
2 teaspoons ground cumin
1 teaspoon hot chili powder
1 teaspoon garam masala
salt and freshly ground black pepper
3lb lean beef, such as rump or top round
3 tablespoons sunflower oil
8 shallots, sliced
4 carrots, thinly sliced
4 stalks celery, thinly sliced
1 rutabaga, cut into small dice
2¼-2¾ cups beef stock
2 tablespoons cornstarch

Preheat the slow cooker on HIGH while preparing the ingredients. Mix spices and seasoning together, add beef, and toss in spice mixture to coat (see above). Heat 2 tablespoons oil in a non-stick skillet, add beef and brown quickly, turning frequently, until sealed all over. Transfer to the cooking pot. Heat remaining oil in the pan, add vegetables, and sauté for 5 minutes; spoon around beef. Add stock to the pan, gently scraping up browned bits in pan using a wooden spoon, and bring to a boil.

Pour enough stock into cooking pot to just cover vegetables. Cover, reduce temperature to LOW, and cook for 6-8 hours or until beef is tender. Remove beef, place on a plate, cover, and keep hot. Transfer vegetable mixture to a pan. In a small bowl, blend cornstarch with a little water until smooth. Stir into vegetable mixture, then bring to a boil, stirring, until thickened. Simmer gently for 3 minutes, stirring. Slice beef and spoon vegetable sauce over. Serve with boiled rice.

Serves 6

CHILI CON CARNE

1 tablespoon sunflower oil
2 red onions, chopped
1 clove garlic, crushed
1 red bell pepper, seeded and chopped
2 fresh red chilies, seeded and finely chopped
1lb 2oz lean ground beef
1 tablespoon all-purpose flour
1 teaspoon ground coriander
1 teaspoon ground cumin
½ teaspoon hot chili powder
⅔ cup beef stock
1¾ cups canned chopped tomatoes
14oz can red kidney beans, rinsed and drained
2 tablespoons tomato paste
salt and freshly ground black pepper
grated Cheddar cheese, to serve (optional)

Preheat the slow cooker on HIGH while preparing the ingredients. Heat the oil in a pan, add the onions, garlic, bell pepper, and chilies and sauté for 5 minutes. Add the ground beef and cook until browned all over, stirring occasionally (see above). Stir in the flour and ground spices and cook for 1 minute, stirring. Add the stock, tomatoes, kidney beans, tomato paste, and seasoning, then bring to a boil, stirring.

Transfer to the cooking pot. Cover, switch the setting to AUTO, and cook for 8-12 hours or until cooked. Serve on a bed of boiled rice and sprinkle with grated cheese, if liked.

Serves 4-6

—— LAMB & APRICOT TAGINE ——

1½lb lean boneless leg or shoulder of lamb
2 tablespoons olive oil
1 large onion, thinly sliced
2 cloves garlic, crushed
4 carrots, thinly sliced
1 tablespoon all-purpose flour
1 teaspoon turmeric
1 teaspoon ground coriander
1 teaspoon ground cumin
1 teaspoon ground cinnamon
salt and freshly ground black pepper
2 cups lamb or vegetable stock
8oz button mushrooms
grated zest of 1 lemon
6oz ready-to-eat dried apricots, chopped
2 tablespoons honey

Preheat the slow cooker on HIGH while preparing the ingredients. Dice the lamb. Heat oil in a pan, add lamb, and cook in batches until sealed all over (see above). Transfer to the cooking pot using a slotted spoon and set aside. Add onion, garlic, and carrots to the pan and sauté for 5 minutes. Stir in flour, ground spices, and seasoning and cook for 1 minute, stirring. Gradually add stock, then add mushrooms and lemon zest and bring to a boil, stirring.

Transfer to the cooking pot and stir to mix. Cover, reduce the temperature to LOW, and cook for 6-8 hours. Stir in apricots and honey, cover, and cook on LOW for a further 1-2 hours, or until the meat is cooked and tender. Serve with couscous and green beans or okra.

Serves 4-6

COOK'S TIP: Sprinkle with chopped fresh cilantro just before serving, if liked.

STEWED LAMB WITH ROSEMARY

2 tablespoons sunflower oil
2¼lb lean boneless leg or shoulder of lamb, diced
12oz button onions or shallots
3 cloves garlic, crushed
8oz button mushrooms
2 tablespoons all-purpose flour
scant 1 cup lamb or vegetable stock
scant 1 cup red wine
1 cup canned chopped tomatoes
1 tablespoon tomato paste
2 tablespoons finely chopped fresh rosemary
salt and freshly ground black pepper
rosemary sprigs, to garnish

Preheat the slow cooker on HIGH while preparing the ingredients. Heat the oil in a pan, add lamb, and cook until sealed all over (see above). Transfer to the cooking pot using a slotted spoon and set aside. Add onions or shallots, garlic, and mushrooms to the pan and sauté for 5 minutes. Stir in flour and cook for 1 minute, stirring.

Gradually add stock and wine, then stir in tomatoes, tomato paste, chopped rosemary, and seasoning. Bring to a boil, stirring, then transfer to the cooking pot and stir to mix. Cover, reduce the temperature to LOW, and cook for 6-8 hours or until the meat is cooked and tender. Garnish with rosemary sprigs. Serve with boiled new potatoes and vegetables such as broccoli and baby carrots.

Serves 4

— LAMB & BELL PEPPER HOTPOT —

2 tablespoons sunflower oil
8 lean loin lamb chops
2 onions, thinly sliced
2 red bell peppers, seeded and sliced
3 stalks celery, thinly sliced
4 carrots, thinly sliced
3 baking potatoes, peeled and thinly sliced
1½ cups lamb or vegetable stock
2 tablespoons tomato paste
2 teaspoons dried mixed herbs
salt and freshly ground black pepper
1 tablespoon butter, melted (optional)
herb sprigs, to garnish

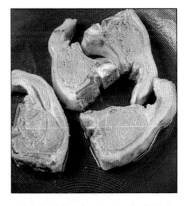

Preheat slow cooker on HIGH while preparing ingredients.

Heat the oil in a pan. Add lamb chops and cook in batches until sealed all over (see above). Transfer to a plate and set aside. Add onions, bell peppers, celery, and carrots to the pan and sauté for 5 minutes. Place 4 lamb chops in the bottom of the cooking pot. Arrange one third of potato slices over the lamb and top potatoes with half of the vegetable mixture. Repeat these layers once again, then finish with a final neat layer of potato slices on top.

Mix stock, tomato paste, dried herbs, and seasoning and pour into cooking pot. Cover, reduce the temperature to LOW, and cook for 8-10 hours or until lamb is cooked and tender. Garnish with herb sprigs and serve with green vegetables.

Serves 4

COOK'S TIP: Use a slow cooker with a capacity of 4.5-5 quarts for best results.

- BRAISED PORK WITH CABBAGE -

1 tablespoon olive oil
2 tablespoons butter
4 lean loin pork chops
1 large onion, thinly sliced
3 stalks celery, finely chopped
2 tablespoons all-purpose flour
generous 1 cup chicken or vegetable stock
generous 1 cup dry or medium cider
3 cups shredded white cabbage
1 large cooking apple, peeled, cored, and sliced
1 teaspoon dried sage
salt and freshly ground black pepper
herb sprigs, to garnish

Preheat the slow cooker on HIGH while preparing the ingredients. Heat oil and butter in a pan. Add chops and cook until sealed all over, turning once. Transfer to the cooking pot using a slotted spoon and set aside (see above). Add onion and celery to the pan and sauté for 5 minutes. Stir in flour and cook for 1 minute, stirring. Gradually stir in stock and cider, then bring to a boil, stirring. Add cabbage, apple, sage, and seasoning and stir to mix.

Spoon the mixture over the chops. Cover, reduce the temperature to LOW, and cook for 6-8 hours, or until the pork is cooked and tender. Garnish with herb sprigs. Serve with mashed potatoes and vegetables such as carrots and petit pois.

Serves 4

VARIATION: Use fresh or dried thyme in place of sage.

—— PORK & BEAN CASSOULET ——

generous 1 cup dried navy beans
3 tablespoons butter
1½lb lean pork tenderloin, diced
1 onion, chopped
1 clove garlic, crushed
2 leeks, washed and thinly sliced
2 stalks celery, sliced
3 carrots, thinly sliced
½ cup all-purpose flour
1 tablespoon paprika
1¼ cups chicken or vegetable stock
scant 1 cup dry or medium cider
1 cup canned chopped tomatoes
1 tablespoon tomato paste
salt and freshly ground black pepper
1 bouquet garni

Place beans in a large bowl. Cover with cold water and leave to soak for at least 10 hours or overnight (see above). Preheat the slow cooker on HIGH while preparing the ingredients. Drain beans, place in a large pan, cover with fresh cold water, and bring to a boil. Boil for 10 minutes, then rinse, drain, and set aside. Meanwhile, melt butter in a pan, add meat and cook until sealed all over. Transfer to the cooking pot using a slotted spoon and set aside. Add onion, garlic, leeks, celery, and carrots to the pan and sauté for 5 minutes.

Stir in flour and paprika and cook for 1 minute, stirring. Gradually stir in stock and cider, then add tomatoes, tomato paste, beans, and seasoning. Bring to a boil, stirring, then add the bouquet garni. Transfer to the cooking pot and stir to mix. Cover, reduce the temperature to LOW, and cook for 8-10 hours, or until the pork is cooked. Remove and discard the bouquet garni. Serve with sautéed potatoes and broccoli flowerets.

Serves 4-6

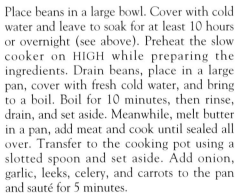

— SWEET & SOUR MEATBALLS —

1lb 2oz lean ground pork
4 shallots, finely chopped
1½ cups finely chopped mushrooms
1 cup fresh bread crumbs
3 tablespoons sun-dried tomato paste
finely grated zest of 1 lemon
2 teaspoons dried herbes de Provence
salt and freshly ground black pepper
2 tablespoons all-purpose flour
2 tablespoons olive oil
1 tablespoon cornstarch
4 tablespoons red wine
1¼ cups canned tomato purée
⅔ cups unsweetened apple juice
2 tablespoons red wine vinegar
2 tablespoons light brown sugar

Place minced pork, shallots, mushrooms, bread crumbs, 2 tablespoons tomato paste, lemon zest, dried herbs, and seasoning in a bowl and mix well (see above). Divide the mixture into 28 equal portions and roll each into a small ball. Roll the meat balls in the flour, place on a plate, and chill in the refrigerator for 20 minutes. Preheat the slow cooker on HIGH. Heat oil in a skillet, add meatballs, and fry for about 10 minutes, or until lightly browned all over, turning occasionally. Meanwhile, blend the cornstarch with the red wine in a pan.

Stir in tomato purée, apple juice, vinegar, sugar, and remaining 1 tablespoon tomato paste. Heat gently, stirring, until the mixture comes to a boil and thickens. Simmer gently for 3 minutes. Transfer the meatballs to the cooking pot using a slotted spoon and pour the sauce over. Cover, reduce the temperature to LOW, and cook for 6-8 hours or until the meatballs are cooked and tender. Serve with cooked egg noodles or rice and stir-fried vegetables.

Serves 4-6

SAUSAGE & MUSHROOM HOTPOT

8 thick spicy pork sausages
2 tablespoons sunflower oil
1 red onion, thinly sliced
1 clove garlic, crushed
1 fresh red chili, seeded and finely chopped
2 parsnips, diced
2 carrots, thinly sliced
2 stalks celery, thinly sliced
4½ cups sliced brown mushrooms
2 tablespoons all-purpose flour
generous 1 cup vegetable stock
scant 1 cup canned tomato purée or tomato juice
2 teaspoons chili sauce
salt and freshly ground black pepper
1½lb peeled potatoes, thinly sliced
1 tablespoon butter, melted (optional)

Preheat the slow cooker on HIGH while preparing the ingredients. Preheat the broiler to medium. Broil sausages until lightly browned all over. Cut each sausage into 3 pieces and set aside (see above). Meanwhile, heat oil in a pan, add onion, garlic, chili, parsnips, carrots, celery, and mushrooms and sauté for 5 minutes. Stir in flour and cook for 1 minute, stirring. Gradually add stock and canned tomato purée or tomato juice, then add chili sauce and seasoning. Bring to a boil, stirring.

Put one third of vegetable mixture in the cooking pot, then arrange one third of potato slices on top. Then add half the sausages. Repeat these layers once again. Top with the remaining vegetable mixture and finish with a final neat layer of potato slices on top. Cover, reduce the temperature to LOW, and cook for 8-10 hours, or until cooked. If desired, brush tops of potatoes with melted butter and place under a preheated broiler until golden. Serve with green beans.

Serves 4-6

— SAUSAGE & LEEK CASSEROLE —

12 thin herbed pork sausages
3 tablespoons butter
1 onion, thinly sliced
3 leeks, washed and thinly sliced
1 clove garlic, crushed
1 butternut squash, peeled, seeded, and cut into
  small dice
3 tablespoons all-purpose flour
1¾ cups vegetable stock
1 cup canned chopped tomatoes
1 tablespoon wholegrain mustard
2 teaspoons chopped fresh thyme
salt and freshly ground black pepper
herb sprigs, to garnish

Preheat the slow cooker on HIGH while preparing the ingredients. Preheat the broiler to medium. Broil sausages until lightly browned all over, then transfer to the cooking pot and set aside (see above). Meanwhile, melt butter in a pan, add onion, leeks, garlic, and squash and sauté for 5 minutes. Stir in flour and cook for 1 minute, stirring. Gradually stir in stock, then add tomatoes, mustard, chopped thyme, and seasoning.

Bring to a boil, stirring, then spoon mixture over sausages. Cover, switch the setting to AUTO and cook for 6-10 hours (or on LOW for 8-10 hours). Garnish with herb sprigs and serve with mashed potatoes, peas, and carrots.

Serves 4

VARIATIONS: Use 1 teaspoon dried thyme in place of fresh thyme. Use half stock and half dry white wine in place of all stock.

HONEY & MUSTARD GLAZED HAM

2¾-3lb uncooked ham
1 onion, quartered
10 black peppercorns
4 bay leaves
1¼ cups medium or dry cider
16 whole cloves (optional)
2 tablespoons light brown sugar
2 tablespoons wholegrain mustard
1 tablespoon honey or marmalade

Place ham in a large bowl, cover with cold water and leave to soak for 3-4 hours, if liked.

Preheat the slow cooker on HIGH while preparing the ingredients. Place ham in a large pan with onion and peppercorns, and cover with fresh cold water. Bring to a boil, then rinse, drain, and place in the cooking pot. Discard onion and peppercorns. Add bay leaves to the cooking pot and pour cider over ham. Cover and cook on HIGH for 4-6 hours, or until ham is cooked and tender. Preheat the oven to 400F (200C). Remove ham from the cooking pot. Discard bay leaves. Remove and discard rind from ham.

Score fat into a diamond pattern. Press cloves into fat, if using, and place ham in a roasting pan. Pour cider and cooking juices round ham. Combine sugar, mustard, and honey or marmalade and spread it over ham. Baste with a little of the cider. Bake for 15-20 minutes or until the glaze is golden and bubbling, basting occasionally. Carve ham into slices and serve hot with parsley sauce and braised vegetables. Or, serve cold with salads and fresh bread.

Serves 6-8

– TUNA & TOMATO CASSEROLE –

2 tablespoons olive oil
1 red onion, thinly sliced
1 yellow bell pepper, seeded and thinly sliced
2 cloves garlic, crushed
2 tablespoons all-purpose flour
scant 1 cup fish or vegetable stock
⅔ cup red or dry white wine
1½lb plum tomatoes, skinned and chopped
8oz button mushrooms, halved
2 zucchini, sliced
salt and freshly ground black pepper
14oz can tuna in brine or spring water
1½ cups drained canned corn kernels
⅔ cup pitted black olives
2 tablespoons chopped fresh mixed herbs

Preheat the slow cooker on HIGH while preparing the ingredients. Heat oil in a pan, add onion, bell peppers, and garlic and sauté for 5 minutes (see above). Stir in flour and cook for 1 minute, stirring. Gradually stir in stock and wine, then add tomatoes, mushrooms, zucchini, and seasoning and bring to a boil, stirring.

Transfer to the cooking pot, cover, and cook on HIGH for 3-4 hours. Drain and flake tuna. Stir tuna, corn, and olives into vegetable sauce, cover and cook on HIGH for a further 1-2 hours, or until the casserole is piping hot. Stir in chopped herbs and serve with cooked pasta such as fusilli or penne.

Serves 6

SALMON & BROCCOLI RISOTTO

2 tablespoons butter
6 shallots, thinly sliced
2 cloves garlic, crushed
1 red bell pepper, seeded and diced
3 cups sliced brown mushrooms
1½ cups quick-cooking rice
1¼ cups dry white wine
2-2¾ cups fish or vegetable stock
salt and freshly ground black pepper
1 cup chopped broccoli flowerets
14oz skinless boneless cooked salmon, flaked
2 tablespoons chopped fresh flat-leaf parsley
fresh Parmesan cheese shavings, to serve

Preheat the slow cooker on HIGH while preparing the ingredients. Melt butter in a pan. Add shallots, garlic, bell pepper, and mushrooms and sauté for 5 minutes. Add rice and cook for 1 minute, stirring (see above). Stir in wine, 2 cups stock and seasoning and bring to a boil. Transfer to the cooking pot, cover, and cook on HIGH for 1-2 hours or until the rice is just cooked and tender and most of the liquid has been absorbed.

Meanwhile, cook broccoli in a pan of boiling water for about 5 minutes or until just tender. Drain well. Stir broccoli and salmon into the risotto, adding a little extra hot stock if required. Cover and cook on HIGH for about 30 minutes, or until salmon is hot and rice is tender. Stir in chopped parsley and sprinkle with Parmesan shavings. Serve with a mixed leaf salad and fresh crusty bread.

Serves 4

COQ AU VIN

2 tablespoons butter
4 chicken portions, skinned
12oz shallots or button onions
2 cloves garlic, crushed
2¼ cups thinly sliced carrots
6oz smoked bacon, diced
¼ cup all-purpose flour
1 cup chicken stock
scant 1 cup red wine
2 tablespoons tomato paste
8oz button mushrooms
salt and freshly ground black pepper
1 bouquet garni
herb sprigs, to garnish

Preheat the slow cooker on HIGH while preparing the ingredients. Melt the butter in a pan. Add chicken portions and cook until lightly browned all over, turning occasionally (see above). Transfer to the cooking pot using a slotted spoon and set aside. Add shallots or button onions, garlic, carrots, and bacon and sauté for 5 minutes. Stir in flour and cook for 1 minute, stirring. Gradually stir in stock and wine, then bring to a boil, stirring.

Add tomato paste, mushrooms, seasoning, and bouquet garni and spoon over the chicken in the cooking pot. Cover and cook on HIGH for 3-5 hours, or until chicken is cooked and tender. Remove and discard the bouquet garni. Garnish with herb sprigs. Serve with boiled egg noodles tossed in melted butter or plain boiled rice.

Serves 4

— CHICKEN & CHICKPEA STEW —

3 tablespoons olive oil
1½lb skinless boneless chicken thighs, diced
8oz shallots, thinly sliced
2 leeks, washed and thinly sliced
1 green or red bell pepper, seeded and thinly sliced
1 yellow bell pepper, seeded and thinly sliced
3 cups sliced brown mushrooms
2 tablespoons all-purpose flour
scant 1 cup dry white wine
⅔ cup chicken stock
1¾ cups canned chopped tomatoes
2 tablespoons sun-dried tomato paste
14-15oz canned chickpeas, rinsed and drained
2 teaspoons dried Italian herb seasoning
salt and freshly ground black pepper
herb sprigs, to garnish

Preheat the slow cooker on HIGH while preparing the ingredients. Heat 2 tablespoons oil in a pan, add the chicken and cook until lightly browned all over. Transfer to the cooking pot using a slotted spoon and set aside (see above). Heat the remaining oil in the pan, add shallots, leeks, bell peppers, and mushrooms and sauté for 5 minutes. Stir in the flour and cook for 1 minute, stirring. Gradually stir in wine and stock, then add tomatoes, tomato paste, chickpeas, dried herbs, and seasoning.

Bring to a boil, stirring, then transfer to the cooking pot and stir to mix. Cover, reduce the temperature to LOW, and cook for 6-8 hours, or until the chicken is cooked and tender. Garnish with herb sprigs and serve with mashed potatoes and green beans.

Serves 6

VARIATION: Use canned red kidney beans in place of chickpeas.

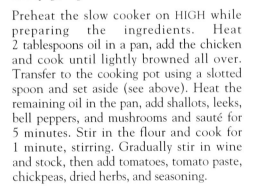

— CHICKEN WITH SHALLOTS —

1 tablespoon olive oil
2 tablespoons butter
4 chicken portions, skinned
1lb shallots, halved
2 cloves garlic, thinly sliced
6oz smoked or unsmoked bacon, diced
2 tablespoons all-purpose flour
1 cup dry white or rosé wine
scant 1 cup chicken stock
6oz button mushrooms
1 tablespoon wholegrain mustard
2 bay leaves
salt and freshly ground black pepper
2 tablespoons chopped fresh flat-leaf parsley

Preheat the slow cooker on HIGH while preparing the ingredients. Heat the oil and butter in a pan, add the chicken, and cook until lightly browned all over. Transfer to the cooking pot using a slotted spoon and set aside (see above). Add shallots, garlic, and bacon to the pan and sauté for 5 minutes. Stir in flour and cook for 1 minute, stirring. Gradually stir in wine and stock, then bring to a boil, stirring.

Add mushrooms, mustard, bay leaves, and seasoning, then pour over chicken in the cooking pot. Cover and cook on HIGH for 3-5 hours, or until the chicken is tender. Remove and discard bay leaves. Sprinkle with parsley and serve with mustard-flavored mashed potatoes and green cabbage.

Serves 4

VARIATIONS: Use button onions in place of shallots. Use Dijon mustard in place of wholegrain mustard.

BARBECUE CHICKEN

3 tablespoons butter
8 chicken drumsticks, skinned
2 red onions, thinly sliced
2 tablespoons all-purpose flour
1¼ cups chicken stock
2 tablespoons tomato paste
4 tablespoons red wine vinegar
4 tablespoons Worcestershire sauce
1 tablespoon dry mustard
salt and freshly ground black pepper
herb sprigs, to garnish

Preheat the slow cooker on HIGH while preparing the ingredients.

Melt the butter in a pan, add chicken drumsticks, and cook until lightly browned all over, turning occasionally. Transfer to the cooking pot using a slotted spoon and set aside. Add onions to the pan and sauté gently for 10 minutes. Stir in flour and cook for 1 minute, stirring. Gradually stir in stock, then add tomato paste, vinegar, Worcestershire sauce, dry mustard, and seasoning.

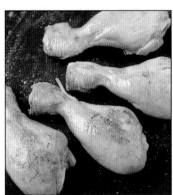

Bring to a boil, stirring, then spoon over the chicken in the cooking pot. Cover and cook on HIGH for 3-5 hours, or until chicken is cooked and tender. Garnish with herb sprigs and serve with roast baby new potatoes and a mixed green salad.

Serves 4

— FRAGRANT CHICKEN CURRY —

3 tablespoons sunflower oil
2 onions, chopped
4 carrots, thinly sliced
2 cloves garlic, crushed
1 fresh green chili, seeded and finely chopped
1 inch piece fresh ginger root, finely chopped
1½lb skinless boneless chicken thighs, diced
2 tablespoons all-purpose flour
2 teaspoons each turmeric, ground coriander, and
   ground cumin
salt and freshly ground black pepper
1¼ cups chicken stock
⅔ cup canned tomato purée
¼ cup golden raisins
⅓ cup toasted cashew nuts
2-3 tablespoons chopped fresh cilantro

Preheat the slow cooker on HIGH while preparing the ingredients. Heat 1 tablespoon oil in a pan, add the onions, carrots, garlic, chili, and ginger and sauté for 5 minutes (see above). Transfer to the cooking pot and set aside. Toss the chicken in flour, ground spices, and seasoning until coated all over. Heat remaining oil in the pan, add chicken in batches and cook quickly until sealed all over. Transfer to the cooking pot.

Add stock and canned tomato purée to the pan and bring to a boil, stirring, scraping up any browned bits in the pan. Add to the cooking pot and stir to mix well. Cover, reduce the temperature to LOW, and cook for 6 hours. Stir in the golden raisins, cover, and cook on LOW for a further 1-2 hours, or until the chicken is cooked and tender. Stir in the cashew nuts and chopped cilantro. Serve with plain boiled rice and a mixed leaf salad.

Serves 4

COUNTRY CHICKEN CASSEROLE

2 tablespoons butter
4 skinless boneless chicken breast halves, each cut
  into 3 pieces
12oz button onions or shallots
2 leeks, washed and thinly sliced
2 stalks celery, thinly sliced
8oz baby carrots
8oz button mushrooms
¼ cup pearl barley
1¾ cups canned chopped tomatoes
2 tablespoons tomato paste
generous 1 cup chicken stock
generous 1 cup dry white wine
salt and freshly ground black pepper
1 bouquet garni
herb sprigs, to garnish

Preheat the slow cooker on HIGH while preparing the ingredients. Melt the butter in a pan, add the chicken, and cook until lightly browned all over, stirring occasionally (see above). Transfer to the cooking pot using a slotted spoon and set aside. Add onions or shallots, leeks, celery, carrots, and mushrooms and sauté for 5 minutes. Stir in pearl barley, tomatoes, tomato paste, stock, wine, and seasoning, then bring to a boil.

Pour over the chicken in the cooking pot and add the bouquet garni. Cover, reduce the temperature to LOW, and cook for 8-10 hours or until the chicken is cooked and tender. Garnish with herb sprigs and serve with mashed potatoes and fresh peas.

Serves 4-6

– ITALIAN CHICKEN CASSOULET –

1 cup dried black-eye peas or cannellini beans
2 tablespoons olive oil
4 chicken portions, skinned
2 large red onions, thinly sliced
2 cloves garlic, crushed
2 red bell peppers, seeded and diced
2 tablespoons all-purpose flour
generous 1 cup chicken stock
⅔ cup red wine
1¼ cups canned chopped tomatoes
3 cups sliced mushrooms
1 tablespoon chopped fresh thyme
1 tablespoon chopped fresh oregano
salt and freshly ground black pepper
herb sprigs, to garnish

Place beans in a large bowl. Cover with cold water and leave to soak for at least 10 hours or overnight (see above). Preheat the slow cooker on HIGH while preparing the ingredients. Drain beans, place in a large pan, cover with fresh cold water, and bring to a boil. Boil for 10 minutes, then rinse, drain, and set aside. Meanwhile, heat oil in a large pan, add chicken portions, and cook until lightly browned all over, turning occasionally. Transfer to the cooking pot and set aside. Add onions, garlic, and bell peppers to the pan and sauté for 5 minutes.

Stir in flour and cook for 1 minute, stirring. Gradually stir in stock and wine, then add tomatoes, mushrooms, chopped herbs, and seasoning. Bring to a boil, stirring, then spoon over chicken in the cooking pot. Cover and cook on HIGH for 2 hours, then reduce the temperature to LOW and cook for a further 4-6 hours, or until the chicken is cooked and tender. Garnish with herb sprigs and serve with warm ciabatta bread and a mixed green salad.

Serves 6

LEMON-BAKED CHICKEN

2 lemons
3lb oven-ready chicken
1 small onion, quartered
2 tablespoons olive oil
⅓ cup butter
2 cloves garlic, thinly sliced
4 tablespoons brandy
2 tablespoons chopped fresh flat-leaf parsley
flat-leaf parsley sprigs, to garnish

Preheat the slow cooker on HIGH while preparing the ingredients. Grate zest and squeeze juice from 1 lemon. Set aside.

Cut remaining lemon into quarters and push into the cavity of the chicken, together with onion quarters. Heat oil and butter in a skillet and quickly brown chicken all over. Transfer chicken to the cooking pot using a slotted spoon and set aside.

Add garlic and lemon zest to the pan and sauté for 3 minutes. Stir lemon juice, brandy, and chopped parsley into the juices in the pan and bring gently to a boil, stirring. Spoon over chicken in the cooking pot, then cover and cook on HIGH for 4-6 hours, or until chicken is cooked and tender. Carve chicken and serve with juices spooned over, if liked. Garnish with parsley sprigs and serve with roast potatoes, baby carrots, and peas.

Serves 4

— CHICKEN TAGINE WITH FIGS —

8 chicken thighs, skinned
1 recipe spice mix (see below)
2 tablespoons olive oil
2 onions, chopped
2 carrots, thinly sliced
2 cloves garlic, crushed
2 teaspoons grated fresh peeled ginger root
6oz button mushrooms, halved
8 large dried figs, roughly chopped
2 tablespoons all-purpose flour
1¾ cups chicken stock
2 tablespoons tomato paste
1 tablespoon lemon juice
⅔ cup black olives
⅓ cup pistachio nuts or 3 tablespoons pine nuts
chopped fresh parsley, to garnish

Preheat slow cooker on HIGH while preparing ingredients. Toss chicken in spice mix until coated (see above). Heat oil in a pan, add chicken, and cook until lightly browned all over, turning occasionally. Transfer to cooking pot using a slotted spoon. Set aside. Add onions, carrots, garlic, and ginger to the pan and sauté for about 5 minutes, or until slightly softened. Add mushrooms and figs, stir in flour, and cook for 1 minute, stirring. Gradually stir in stock, tomato paste, and lemon juice. Bring slowly to a boil, stirring, then pour over chicken. Stir gently to mix.

Cover and cook on HIGH for 3-5 hours (or on MEDIUM for 4-6 hours) or until the chicken is tender. About 1 hour before serving, stir in olives and nuts. Garnish with parsley.

Serves 4

SPICE MIX: In a bowl, combine 2 tablespoons olive oil, 2 teaspoons ground coriander, 2 teaspoons ground cumin, 1½ teaspoons ground cinnamon, 1½ teaspoons turmeric, finely grated zest and juice of ½ lemon, and 1½ teaspoons harissa paste.

—— POUSSIN BRAISED IN WINE ——

4 poussin, about 12oz each
1 lemon, cut into quarters
few sprigs of cilantro
3 tablespoons butter
2 leeks, washed and sliced
⅔ cup red wine
2 tablespoons honey
salt and freshly ground black pepper
1 tablespoon cornstarch
cilantro sprigs, to garnish

Preheat the slow cooker on HIGH while preparing the ingredients. Stuff each poussin with one quarter of lemon and a sprig or two of cilantro.

Melt the butter in a skillet and quickly brown the birds all over. Transfer them to the cooking pot, using a slotted spoon. Set aside. Add the leeks to the pan and sauté for 5 minutes, then add wine, honey, and seasoning and bring to a boil, stirring. Spoon over the poussin in the cooking pot. Cover and cook on HIGH for 4-6 hours, or until poussin are cooked and tender. Remove poussin from the cooking pot, place on a plate, and keep hot.

In a small pan, blend the cornstarch with a little water. Stir in red wine sauce from the cooking pot, then bring to a boil, stirring, until thickened. Simmer gently for 3 minutes, stirring. Serve the poussin with the wine and leek sauce spooned over. Garnish with cilantro sprigs and serve with creamy mashed potatoes and stir-fried green vegetables.

Serves 4

TURKEY & MUSHROOM RISOTTO

½oz dried porcini mushrooms
2 tablespoons sunflower oil
6 shallots, thinly sliced
1 clove garlic, crushed
3 stalks celery, finely chopped
8oz skinless boneless turkey breast, cut into small
  pieces
1½ cups quick-cooking rice
3 cups sliced mixed fresh wild mushrooms
1¼ cups dry white wine
2-2¾ cups chicken stock
salt and freshly ground black pepper
1½ cups drained canned corn kernels
2 tablespoons chopped fresh mixed herbs
grated fresh Parmesan, for sprinkling

Preheat the slow cooker on HIGH while preparing the ingredients. Place the dried mushrooms in a small bowl, pour over ½ cup boiling water and leave to soak for 20 minutes. Drain mushrooms, reserving soaking liquid, then snip into small pieces using scissors. Set aside (see above). Heat the oil in a pan, add the shallots, garlic, and celery and sauté for 5 minutes. Add turkey and cook until lightly browned all over, stirring frequently. Add rice and fresh and soaked mushrooms and cook for 1 minute, stirring.

Add wine, 2 cups of the stock, the reserved mushroom liquid, and seasoning and bring to a boil. Transfer to the cooking pot. Cover and cook on HIGH for 1 hour. Stir in corn kernels and add a little extra hot stock, if needed. Cover and cook on HIGH for a further 30-60 minutes, or until turkey and rice are cooked and tender and all the liquid has been absorbed. Stir in chopped herbs and sprinkle with Parmesan. Serve with crusty bread and a mixed leaf salad.

Serves 4-6

CURRIED TURKEY WITH COCONUT

2 tablespoons olive oil
1 onion, chopped
2 cloves garlic, crushed
1 green bell pepper, seeded and thinly sliced
1lb 2oz skinless boneless turkey meat, cut into small
   dice
1 teaspoon ground coriander
1 teaspoon ground cumin
4 teaspoons green Thai curry paste
4oz green beans, halved
6oz baby corn, halved
1¼ cups chicken stock
⅔ cup coconut milk
2 tablespoons cornstarch
2-3 tablespoons chopped fresh cilantro
toasted flaked coconut, to garnish

Preheat the slow cooker on HIGH while preparing the ingredients. Heat the oil in a pan, add onion, garlic, bell pepper, and turkey and sauté for about 5 minutes, or until the turkey is browned all over, stirring occasionally (see above). Add ground spices and curry paste, and cook for 1 minute, stirring. Add green beans, corn, stock, and coconut milk and stir to mix.

In a small bowl, blend the cornstarch with a little water, add to the curry, and stir well to mix. Bring to a boil, stirring, then transfer to the cooking pot. Cover, reduce the temperature to LOW, and cook for 6-8 hours, or until turkey is cooked and tender. Stir in chopped cilantro and garnish with toasted flaked coconut. Serve with plain boiled rice.

Serves 4

– BRAISED DUCK WITH ORANGE –

2 tablespoons butter
4 duck portions, skinned
2 red onions, thinly sliced
3 cups sliced brown mushrooms
2 tablespoons all-purpose flour
seeds from 4 cardamom pods, crushed
¾ cup chicken stock
⅔ cup red wine
grated zest and juice of 1 orange
2 tablespoons orange marmalade
salt and freshly ground black pepper
herb sprigs, to garnish

Preheat the slow cooker on HIGH while preparing the ingredients.

Melt the butter in a pan. Add the duck and cook until lightly browned all over, turning occasionally. Transfer to the cooking pot using a slotted spoon and set aside. Add onions and mushrooms to the pan and sauté for 5 minutes. Stir in flour and cardamom and cook for 1 minute, stirring. Gradually stir in stock and wine, then add orange zest and juice, marmalade, and seasoning.

Bring to a boil, stirring, then spoon over the duck in the cooking pot. Cover and cook on HIGH for 3-5 hours, or until duck is cooked and tender. Garnish with herb sprigs and serve with boiled new potatoes, snow peas, and baby corn.

Serves 4

VENISON CASSEROLE

2 tablespoons sunflower oil
1½lb lean stewing venison, cut into small dice
2 red onions, thinly sliced
4 carrots, thinly sliced
3 stalks celery, thinly sliced
3 tablespoons all-purpose flour
1 cup game or chicken stock
scant 1 cup red wine
7oz button mushrooms
1 cup dried cranberries
2 tablespoons cranberry sauce
1 tablespoon chopped fresh thyme
salt and freshly ground black pepper
herb sprigs, to garnish

Preheat the slow cooker on HIGH while preparing the ingredients. Heat the oil in a large pan, add venison, and cook until browned all over, stirring occasionally (see above). Transfer to the cooking pot using a slotted spoon and set aside. Add onions, carrots, and celery to the pan and sauté for 5 minutes. Stir in flour and cook for 1 minute, stirring. Gradually stir in stock and wine, then add mushrooms, dried cranberries, cranberry sauce, chopped thyme, and seasoning and bring to a boil, stirring.

Transfer to the cooking pot and stir to mix well. Cover, reduce the temperature to LOW, and cook for 8-10 hours, or until the venison is cooked and tender. Garnish with herb sprigs and serve with mustard-flavored mashed potatoes and broccoli flowerets.

Serves 4-6

VARIATION: Use lean round steak in place of venison.

STUFFED BELL PEPPERS

4 large bell peppers (assorted colors)
2 tablespoons olive oil
4 shallots, finely chopped
1 clove garlic, crushed
1½ cups finely chopped mushrooms
1 zucchini, finely chopped
1 cup cooked brown rice
2 tomatoes, skinned, seeded and finely chopped
4 tablespoons pine nuts, finely chopped
⅓ cup pitted black olives, finely chopped
2 tablespoons chopped fresh mixed herbs
salt and freshly ground black pepper
⅔ cup vegetable stock

Preheat the slow cooker on HIGH while preparing the ingredients. Slice the tops off the bell peppers and remove and discard cores and seeds (see above). Cook bell peppers and lids in a pan of boiling water for 5 minutes. Drain well and set aside. Heat oil in a pan, add shallots, garlic, mushrooms, and zucchini and sauté for 5 minutes. Remove the pan from the heat and stir in all the remaining ingredients, except stock, and mix well.

Spoon some rice stuffing into each bell pepper and top with the lids. Place in the cooking pot. Heat stock in a pan until boiling, then pour it around the bell peppers. Cover and cook on HIGH for 2-4 hours, or until bell peppers are tender. Serve with fresh crusty bread and a mixed baby leaf salad.

Serves 4

── RATATOUILLE BEANPOT ──

3 tablespoons olive oil
1 large onion, thinly sliced
2 cloves garlic, crushed
1 eggplant, cut into small dice
1 each green, red and yellow bell pepper, seeded and
   thinly sliced
2 zucchini, sliced
1¾ cups canned chopped tomatoes
5 tablespoons dry white wine or vegetable stock
1 tablespoon tomato paste
2 teaspoons dried herbes de Provence
2 cups rinsed and drained canned red kidney beans
2 cups rinsed and drained canned black-eyed peas
salt and freshly ground black pepper
herb sprigs, to garnish

Preheat the slow cooker on HIGH while preparing the ingredients. Heat the oil in a large pan, add the onion, garlic, eggplant, and bell peppers and sauté for 5 minutes (see above). Add the zucchini, tomatoes, wine or stock, tomato paste, dried herbs, beans, black-eyed peas, and seasoning and stir to mix well.

Bring to a boil, stirring occasionally, then transfer to the cooking pot. Cover, reduce the temperature to LOW, and cook for 6-8 hours or until the vegetables are tender. Garnish with herb sprigs and serve with fresh crusty bread. Sprinkle the ratatouille with a little grated Cheddar or Gruyère cheese, if liked.

Serves 4-6

– MACARONI & BROCCOLI BAKE –

1⅔ cups dried macaroni
1 cup chopped broccoli flowerets
⅓ cup butter
8oz leeks, washed and thinly sliced
½ cup all-purpose flour
4 cups milk
1¼ cups grated Cheddar cheese
1 teaspoon prepared English mustard
1½ cups drained canned corn kernels
salt and freshly ground black pepper
½ cup fresh bread crumbs (optional)
¼ cup finely grated fresh Parmesan cheese (optional)
2 tablespoons chopped fresh chives (optional)

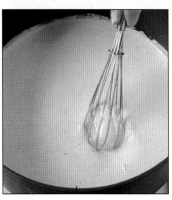

Preheat the slow cooker on HIGH while preparing ingredients. Cook macaroni in a pan of boiling water for 8 minutes, or until just tender. Add broccoli for last 3 minutes of cooking (see above). Drain well and set aside. Melt 2 tablespoons of the butter in a pan, add leeks, and sauté for 8-10 minutes, or until softened. Place on a plate and set aside. Add remaining butter to the pan with flour and milk and heat gently, whisking, until the sauce comes to a boil and thickens. Simmer gently for 3 minutes, stirring.

Remove the pan from the heat and stir in cheese until it has melted. Add macaroni, broccoli, leeks, mustard, corn, and seasoning and mix well. Grease cooking pot of slow cooker. Transfer the macaroni mixture to the cooking pot. Cover, reduce temperature to LOW, and cook for 3-4 hours. If desired, preheat the broiler to high; combine bread crumbs, Parmesan, and chives and sprinkle over the top. Broil until golden. Serve with broiled tomatoes and a salad.

Serves 6

—ROOT VEGETABLE CASSEROLE—

2 tablespoons olive oil
1 onion, thinly sliced
1 clove garlic, crushed
3 stalks celery, thinly sliced
1½ cups thinly sliced carrots
1¼ cups peeled diced rutabaga
1 cup peeled diced parsnips
2 cups peeled diced potatoes
2 teaspoons each of ground coriander, ground cumin,
   and hot chili powder
1 cup puy or green lentils, rinsed and drained
1¾ cups canned chopped tomatoes
3 cups vegetable stock
salt and freshly ground black pepper
2 tablespoons chopped fresh cilantro

Preheat the slow cooker on HIGH while preparing the ingredients. Heat the oil in a large pan, add onion, garlic, and celery and sauté for 3 minutes. Add carrots, rutabaga, parsnips, and potatoes and sauté for 5 minutes (see above). Add ground spices and cook for 1 minute, stirring. Add lentils, tomatoes, stock, and seasoning and stir to mix. Bring to a boil, stirring, then transfer to the cooking pot.

Cover and cook on HIGH for 3-4 hours or until the vegetables and lentils are cooked and tender. Stir in chopped cilantro and serve with fresh crusty bread.

Serves 4-6

VARIATIONS: Use 4-6 shallots in place of onion. Use sweet potatoes in place of standard potatoes.

—— VEGETABLE CHILI BAKE ——

2 tablespoons sunflower oil
6 shallots, sliced
2 cloves garlic, crushed
3 stalks celery, finely chopped
1 green bell pepper, seeded and diced
1 large fresh green chili, seeded and finely chopped
3 carrots, thinly sliced
1 cup peeled diced turnip or rutabaga
2 teaspoons ground cumin
1 teaspoon hot chili powder
1¾ cups canned chopped tomatoes
2 tablespoons tomato paste
scant 1 cup vegetable stock
3 cups sliced brown mushrooms
2 cups rinsed and drained canned red kidney beans
salt and freshly ground black pepper
1 tablespoon cornstarch

Preheat the slow cooker on HIGH while preparing the ingredients. Heat the oil in a pan, add shallots, garlic, celery, bell pepper, and chili and sauté for 3 minutes (see above). Add carrots and turnip or rutabaga and sauté for 5 minutes. Add the ground spices and cook for 1 minute, stirring. Add tomatoes, tomato paste, stock, mushrooms, kidney beans, and seasoning and stir to mix. In a small bowl, blend the cornstarch with a little water, then stir it into the vegetable mixture.

Bring to a boil, stirring, then transfer to the cooking pot. Cover, reduce the temperature to LOW, and cook for 6-8 hours, or until the vegetables are cooked and tender. Garnish with herb sprigs, if you like, and serve on a bed of plain cooked rice.

Serves 4

VARIATION: Use 1 brown or red onion in place of shallots. Use closed cup or button mushrooms in place of brown mushrooms.

— CHEESY ZUCCHINI STRATA —

2 tablespoons butter
1 onion, finely chopped
1 small leek, washed and thinly sliced
2 zucchini, sliced
1 cup drained canned corn kernels
salt and freshly ground black pepper
9 medium slices of bread, crusts removed and slices
   cut into strips
3 eggs
1½ cups hot milk
2 tablespoons chopped fresh chives
2 tablespoons chopped fresh parsley
¾ cup grated mature Cheddar cheese

Preheat the slow cooker on HIGH while preparing the ingredients. Grease a 1- to 2-quart ovenproof soufflé or similar dish and set aside (see above). Melt the butter in a pan, add onion, leek, and zucchini and sauté for 8-10 minutes or until softened. Remove the pan from the heat and stir in corn and seasoning. Set aside. Place one third of the bread strips in the base of the prepared dish. Top with half the zucchini mixture. Repeat the layers, ending with a layer of bread.

Whisk together eggs, hot milk, chopped herbs, and seasoning, then pour into the dish over the bread and vegetables. Sprinkle the cheese on top. Cover loosely with greased foil. Place in the cooking pot of the slow cooker. Add sufficient boiling water to the cooking pot to come halfway up the sides of the dish. Cover and cook on HIGH for 3-4 hours (or on LOW for 4-6 hours) or until lightly set. Serve with broccoli and cauliflower flowerets or a mixed leaf salad.

Serves 4-6

VEGETABLE RAGOÛT

2 tablespoons olive oil
1 onion, chopped
1 clove garlic, finely chopped
2 carrots, thinly sliced
2 stalks celery, finely chopped
1 green bell pepper, seeded and diced
1 yellow bell pepper, seeded and diced
6oz baby corn, halved
8oz button mushrooms
2 tablespoons butter
¼ cup all-purpose flour
1¼ cups canned tomato purée
⅔ cup medium or dry cider
2 teaspoons dried mixed herbs
salt and freshly ground black pepper
herb sprigs, to garnish

Preheat the slow cooker on HIGH while preparing the ingredients. Heat the oil in a pan, add onion, garlic, carrots, celery, bell peppers, and corn and sauté for 5 minutes (see above). Transfer to the cooking pot with mushrooms and set aside. Add butter to the pan and heat until melted. Stir in flour and cook for 1 minute, stirring. Gradually stir in canned tomato purée, and cider, then heat gently, stirring continuously, until the sauce comes to a boil and thickens. Simmer gently for 2 minutes, stirring.

Stir in the dried herbs and seasoning, then spoon over vegetables in the cooking pot and stir to mix well. Cover, reduce the temperature to LOW, and cook for 6-8 hours, or until vegetables are cooked and tender. Garnish with herb sprigs. Serve with mashed potatoes flavored with scallions and a mixed baby leaf salad.

Serves 4

VARIATION: Use vegetable stock or wine in place of cider.

– HARVEST VEGETABLE HOTPOT –

2 tablespoons sunflower oil
6 shallots, sliced
2 leeks, washed and sliced
2 stalks celery, finely chopped
1 red bell pepper, seeded and sliced
1lb prepared mixed root vegetables such as carrots,
  parsnips, and rutabaga or turnip, diced
¾ cup chopped cauliflower flowerets
1¼ cups canned chopped tomatoes
⅔ cup vegetable stock
⅔ cup dry white wine or cider
2 teaspoons dried herbes de Provence
salt and freshly ground black pepper
2 tablespoons cornstarch
1lb peeled potatoes, thinly sliced
1 tablespoon butter, melted (optional)

Preheat the slow cooker on HIGH while
preparing the ingredients. Heat the oil in a
large pan, add shallots, leeks, and celery and
sauté for 5 minutes (see above). Add red bell
pepper, root vegetables, and cauliflower and
sauté for a further 5 minutes. Add tomatoes,
stock, wine or cider, dried herbs, and
seasoning and mix well. In a small bowl,
blend cornstarch with a little water, then stir
into vegetable mixture. Bring to a boil,
stirring continuously, until the mixture
thickens. Simmer gently for 2 minutes,
stirring.

Spoon one third of the vegetable mixture
into the cooking pot, then arrange one third
of the potato slices on top. Repeat these
layers twice more, finishing with a neat layer
of potatoes on top. Cover, reduce the
temperature to LOW, and cook for 6-8 hours,
or until the vegetables are cooked and
tender. Garnish with herb sprigs, if you like,
and serve with green beans.

Serves 4-6

ROOT VEGETABLE CURRY

2 tablespoons olive oil
1 red onion, chopped
2 cloves garlic, crushed
1 fresh red chili, seeded and finely chopped
1 inch piece fresh ginger root, peeled and finely chopped
1½lb mixed root vegetables such as sweet potato, potato, carrots, celeriac and rutabaga, diced
2 tablespoons all-purpose flour
2 teaspoons each of ground turmeric, ground coriander, and ground cumin
1½ cups vegetable stock
⅔ cup canned tomato purée
¾ cup golden raisins
salt and freshly ground black pepper
2-3 tablespoons chopped fresh cilantro

Preheat the slow cooker on HIGH while preparing the ingredients. Heat the oil in a large pan, add onion, garlic, chili, and ginger and sauté for 3 minutes (see above). Add root vegetables and sauté gently for 10 minutes. Stir in flour and ground spices and cook for 1 minute, stirring. Gradually stir in the stock and canned tomato purée, then add the golden raisins and seasoning.

Bring to a boil, stirring, then transfer to the cooking pot. Cover, reduce the temperature to LOW, and cook for 8-10 hours, or until the vegetables are cooked and tender. Stir in the chopped cilantro and serve with plain boiled rice.

Serves 4

VARIATIONS: Use brown onion in place of red onion. Use tomato juice in place of canned tomato purée.

FRUIT & NUT PILAF

1 tablespoon olive oil
1 onion, finely chopped
2 cloves garlic, crushed
1 fresh red chili, seeded and finely chopped
1 red bell pepper, seeded and diced
1½ teaspoons ground coriander
1½ teaspoons ground cumin
1½ cups quick-cooking rice
⅔ cup golden raisins
1 cup chopped ready-to-eat dried apricots
3 cups vegetable stock, plus extra if needed
3 tablespoons dry sherry
salt and freshly ground black pepper
¾ cup unsalted cashew nuts, toasted
2 tablespoons chopped fresh cilantro
cilantro sprigs, to garnish

Preheat the slow cooker on HIGH while preparing the ingredients. Heat the oil in a pan, add onion, garlic, chili, and bell pepper and sauté for 5 minutes (see above). Add the ground spices and rice and cook for 1 minute, stirring. Add golden raisins, apricots, stock, sherry, and seasoning and mix well.

Bring to a boil, stirring, then transfer to the cooking pot. Cover and cook on HIGH for 1-2 hours, or until rice is cooked and tender and all the liquid has been absorbed. Stir once halfway through the cooking time and add a little extra hot stock, if needed. Stir in cashew nuts and chopped cilantro. Garnish with cilantro sprigs and serve with a mixed green salad.

Serves 4

—— BARBECUE BAKED BEANS ——

1¼ cups dried navy beans
1 tablespoon sunflower oil
1 red onion, finely chopped
2 cloves garlic, crushed
2 stalks celery, finely chopped
1¾ cups canned chopped tomatoes
1¼ cups vegetable stock
4 tablespoons red wine vinegar
2 tablespoons Worcestershire sauce
2 tablespoons light brown sugar
2 tablespoons tomato paste
1 tablespoon Dijon mustard
salt and freshly ground black pepper

Place the beans in a large bowl. Cover with plenty of cold water and leave to soak for at least 10 hours or overnight (see above). Preheat the slow cooker on HIGH while preparing the ingredients. Drain beans, place in a large pan, cover with fresh cold water, and bring to a boil. Boil for 10 minutes, then rinse, drain, and set aside. Heat oil in a pan, add onion, garlic, and celery and sauté for 5 minutes. Add tomatoes, stock, vinegar, Worcestershire sauce, sugar, tomato paste, mustard, seasoning, and beans and mix well.

Bring to a boil, stirring occasionally, then transfer to the cooking pot. Cover, reduce the temperature to LOW, and cook for 8-12 hours or until beans are tender. Serve with crusty French bread and a mixed leaf salad.

Serves 4-6

COOK'S TIP: To thicken the sauce, transfer cooked beans and sauce to a pan. Blend 1-2 tablespoons cornstarch with a little water, then stir it into the mixture. Bring to a boil, stirring, then simmer gently for 3 minutes.

MEDITERRANEAN VEGETABLE STEW

2 tablespoons olive oil
2 red onions, thinly sliced
2 cloves garlic, crushed
2 yellow bell peppers, seeded and thinly sliced
3 zucchini, sliced
8oz button mushrooms, halved
1lb plum tomatoes, skinned and sliced
4 tablespoons red wine
2 tablespoons sun-dried tomato paste
salt and freshly ground black pepper
2 tablespoons chopped fresh basil
2 tablespoons chopped fresh flat-leaf parsley
fresh Parmesan cheese shavings, to serve

Preheat the slow cooker on HIGH while preparing the ingredients. Heat the oil in a large pan, add onions, garlic, and bell peppers and sauté for 5 minutes. Add zucchini, mushrooms, tomatoes, wine, tomato paste, and seasoning, then bring to a boil, stirring.

Transfer to the cooking pot, cover, reduce the temperature to LOW, and cook for 6-8 hours, or until the vegetables are cooked and tender. Stir in chopped herbs and sprinkle with Parmesan shavings. Serve with warm ciabatta bread.

Serves 4

VARIATIONS: Use brown onions in place of red onions. Use red bell peppers in place of yellow bell peppers.

—— WINTER FRUIT COMPOTE ——

1⅓ cups ready-to-eat dried apricots
½ cup dried apple rings
⅔ cup ready-to-eat dried prunes
⅓ cup golden raisins
⅓ cup dark raisins
1 pear, peeled, cored and cut into 8
2 cinnamon sticks
thinly pared zest of 1 lemon
2¾ cups unsweetened apple juice
mint sprigs, to decorate

Preheat the slow cooker on HIGH for 15-20 minutes. Put all the dried fruit and the pear in the cooking pot.

Add cinnamon sticks, lemon zest, and apple juice and stir gently to mix. Cover, reduce the temperature to LOW, and cook for 8-10 hours or until the fruit is plumped up and tender.

Remove and discard cinnamon sticks and lemon zest. Decorate with mint sprigs. Serve the compote warm or cold with heavy cream, mascarpone cheese, or Greek-style yogurt.

Serves 6

VARIATION: Use your own choice of mixed dried fruits in similar proportions to above, if preferred.

CHOCOLATE FONDUE

12oz dark chocolate
3 tablespoons butter
1 cup heavy cream
½ teaspoon ground cinnamon
3 tablespoons brandy or rum
selection of prepared fresh fruit such as strawberries,
   cherries, kiwi fruit, and banana, for dipping
ladyfingers or thin cookies, for dipping
ready-to-eat dried fruits such as apricots and figs and
   whole nuts such as walnuts or brazil nuts, for
   dipping

Break the chocolate into squares.

Place chocolate squares in the cooking pot
of the slow cooker with the butter, cream,
cinnamon, and brandy or rum. Stir to mix.
Cover and cook on LOW for 1-2 hours, or
until all the ingredients have melted
together, stirring once.

Stir briskly until well combined and
smooth, then serve with the fresh and dried
fruits, ladyfingers, and nuts for dipping.

Serves 6-8

APRICOT BREAD PUDDING

3 tablespoons butter, softened
6 medium slices of bread, crusts removed
1½ cups finely chopped ready-to-eat dried apricots
3 tablespoons light brown sugar
2 teaspoons ground mixed spice
3 extra large eggs
2 cups light cream

Preheat the slow cooker on HIGH while preparing the ingredients. Lightly grease a 7- to 8-cup ovenproof soufflé or similar dish that will sit in your cooking pot, and set aside.

Spread the butter over the bread slices, then cut bread into small triangles or fingers. Arrange half the bread in the base of the prepared dish, butter-side up. Mix together apricots, sugar, and mixed spice and sprinkle over bread. Top with remaining bread, butter-side up. Beat the eggs and cream together and pour over bread. Set aside for 30 minutes to allow the bread to absorb some of the liquid.

Cover with greased foil, then place in the cooking pot of the slow cooker. Add sufficient boiling water to the cooking pot to come halfway up the sides of the dish. Cover, reduce the temperature to LOW, and cook for 3-5 hours or until set. Serve with fresh fruit such as sliced peaches, nectarines, or apricots.

Serves 4-6

VARIATION: Use golden raisins or dried pears in place of apricots. Use ground cinnamon or ginger in place of mixed spice.

RHUBARB WITH ORANGE & GINGER

1½lb rhubarb, trimmed
6 tablespoons light brown sugar
finely grated zest and juice of 1 orange
scant ½ cup freshly squeezed orange juice
3 tablespoons preserved stem ginger syrup
1 teaspoon ground mixed spice
2-3 pieces preserved stem ginger, finely chopped

Preheat the slow cooker on HIGH while preparing the ingredients. Cut the rhubarb into 1 inch lengths and place in the cooking pot.

Add the sugar and orange zest and stir to mix. Mix orange juices, syrup, and mixed spice together, pour over rhubarb and stir to mix. Cover, reduce the temperature to LOW, and cook for 4-6 hours or until rhubarb is tender.

Stir in chopped stem ginger and extra sugar, if required. Serve warm or cold with custard, ice cream, or heavy cream.

Serves 4

VARIATIONS: Use plums, pitted and halved, in place of rhubarb. Use ground ginger or cinnamon in place of mixed spice.

FRESH LEMON SPONGE PUDDING

4 tablespoons corn syrup
½ cup butter (softened) or margarine
¾ cup light brown sugar
2 eggs
finely grated zest of 1 lemon
1½ cups self-rising flour, sifted
2-3 tablespoons milk

Preheat the slow cooker on HIGH while preparing the ingredients. Lightly grease a 4½-cup pudding basin and line the base with a small circle of non-stick baking paper. Spoon the syrup into the base of the prepared basin and set aside.

In a bowl, beat the butter or margarine and sugar together until pale and creamy. Gradually beat in eggs, then beat in lemon zest. Fold in flour, adding enough milk to make a soft, dropping consistency. Spoon the mixture into the basin over the syrup and level the surface. Cover loosely with a double layer of greased foil and place in the cooking pot of the slow cooker.

Add sufficient boiling water to the cooking pot to come halfway up the sides of the basin. Cover and cook on HIGH for 3-4 hours or until the sponge is cooked and a skewer inserted in the center comes out clean. Carefully turn out on to a warmed serving plate and serve with custard, cream, or ice cream.

Serves 6

FESTIVE PLUM PUDDING

1 cup dark raisins
1 cup golden raisins
½ cup dried cranberries
½ cup finely chopped ready-to-eat dried apricots
finely grated zest and juice of 1 small orange
finely grated zest and juice of 1 lemon
2 tablespoons brandy or sherry
½ cup all-purpose flour
2 teaspoons ground mixed spice
2 cups fresh bread crumbs
4oz shredded beef suet or vegetable shortening
¾ cup light brown sugar
3 eggs, beaten

Put dried fruit, fruit zests and juices, and brandy or sherry in a bowl and stir to mix.

Cover and leave to soak for several hours or overnight. Preheat the slow cooker on HIGH. Lightly grease a 6- to 6½-cup pudding basin and line the base with a circle of waxed paper. Set aside. Mix flour, mixed spice, bread crumbs, suet, and sugar in a bowl. Add dried fruits with soaking liquid and eggs and beat together until thoroughly mixed. Spoon the mixture into the prepared basin and level the surface. Cover with a sheet of waxed paper and a double layer of pleated foil. Secure with string.

Place in the cooking pot of the slow cooker. Add sufficient boiling water to the pot to come three-quarters of the way up the sides of the basin. Cover and cook on HIGH for 8-12 hours, or until cooked, topping up with boiling water as necessary. Remove the pudding from the slow cooker, turn out on to a warmed serving plate, and serve immediately or allow to cool, then re-cover and store in a cool place until required. Serve with brandy butter or cream.

Serves 8-10

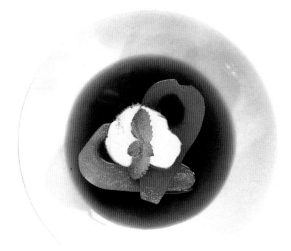

TIPSY PEARS

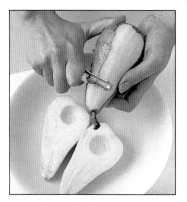

4 large Bosc pears
scant 2 cups red wine
⅔ cup unsweetened apple juice
½ cup light brown sugar
2 cinnamon sticks
4 whole cloves
mint sprigs, to decorate

Preheat the slow cooker on HIGH while preparing the ingredients. Carefully peel the pears, then cut them in half and remove and discard cores. Place in the cooking pot and set aside.

Place the red wine, apple juice, and sugar in a saucepan and heat gently, stirring, until the sugar has dissolved. Add cinnamon sticks and cloves, then bring to a boil. Pour over pears in the cooking pot. Cover, reduce the temperature to LOW, and cook for 6-8 hours or until pears are tender.

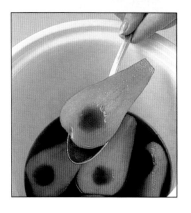

Carefully remove pears from the liquid and keep hot. Remove and discard the cinnamon sticks and cloves. Pour the liquid into a pan and boil rapidly until it is reduced and thickened slightly. Spoon the liquid over the pears and decorate with mint sprigs. Serve warm or cold with heavy cream or Greek-style yogurt.

Serves 4

— RICE PUDDING WITH ORANGE —

2 tablespoons butter
½ cup short-grain rice, rinsed and drained
⅓ cup superfine sugar
3 cups milk
1 cup evaporated milk
finely grated zest of 1 large orange
seeds from 3 cardamom pods, crushed
pared orange zest, to decorate

Grease the inside of the cooking pot of the slow cooker with a little of the butter.

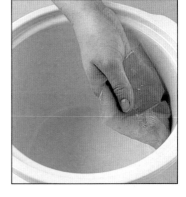

Place the rice, sugar, milk, evaporated milk, orange zest, and crushed cardamom seeds in the cooking pot and stir to mix.

Dot with any remaining butter. Cover and cook on HIGH for 3-4 hours (or on LOW for 4-6 hours) or until the rice is cooked and most of the liquid has been absorbed, stirring once or twice during the final 2 hours of cooking, if possible. Decorate with pared orange zest. Serve with stewed fresh fruit such as plums or warm fruit compote.

Serves 4-6

CREAMY LEMON RICE DESSERT

2 tablespoons butter
¼ cup short-grain rice, rinsed and drained
2 cups milk
⅔ cup evaporated milk
finely grated zest of 1 lemon
2 tablespoons plus 2 teaspoons superfine sugar
4-6 tablespoons heavy cream
pared lemon and orange zest, to decorate
1½ cups sliced strawberries, to serve

Lightly grease the cooking pot of the slow cooker with a little of the butter. Cut the remaining butter into small pieces.

Put the butter pieces, rice, milk, evaporated milk, lemon zest and sugar in the cooking pot and stir to mix. Cover and cook on LOW for 4-6 hours (or on HIGH for 3-4 hours) or until rice is cooked and most of the liquid has been absorbed, stirring once or twice during the final 2 hours of cooking, if possible. Transfer the mixture to a bowl and allow to cool. Once cold, remove and discard any skin from the top surface, then chill.

Fold the heavy cream into the lemon rice and decorate with pared lemon and orange zest. Serve with sliced strawberries.

Serves 4

VARIATION: Use 2¾ cups milk in place of mixture of milk and evaporated milk, if preferred. This dessert may also be served warm. Simply fold the heavy cream into the warm lemon rice and serve with strawberries.

— CINNAMON BAKED APPLES —

2 tablespoons butter
4 large cooking apples
¼ cup dried cherries, chopped
¼ cup dried cranberries
2 tablespoons light brown sugar
2 tablespoons honey
2 teaspoons ground cinnamon
4 tablespoons unsweetened apple juice
extra sugar or honey, to sweeten (optional)

Preheat the slow cooker on HIGH while preparing the ingredients. Lightly grease the cooking pot with a little of the butter. Set aside.

Wash and dry apples but do not peel them. Remove apple cores using a corer, then make a shallow cut through the skin around each apple. In a small bowl, mix together dried cherries, cranberries, sugar, honey, and cinnamon. Fill the apple cavities with the fruit mixture. Stand apples in the cooking pot and dot with remaining butter (see below). Spoon the apple juice around apples.

Cover, reduce the temperature to LOW, and cook for 3-6 hours, or until cooked and tender. Serve on warmed serving plates and sweeten with extra sugar or honey, if liked. Serve with ice cream or heavy cream.

Serves 4

COOK'S TIP: The juices from the cooked apples may be boiled rapidly in a pan until reduced and thickened, then spooned over apples, if liked.

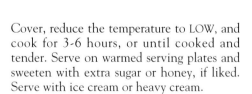

— DATE & WALNUT PUDDING —

FOR THE PUDDING:
¾ cup butter (softened) or margarine
1 cup light brown sugar
2 eggs, beaten
1½ cups self-rising flour, sifted
⅓ cup chopped dried pitted dates
½ cup walnuts, chopped
about 2 tablespoons milk
FOR THE CHOCOLATE FUDGE SAUCE:
6oz dark chocolate, broken into squares
scant ½ cup heavy cream
⅓ cup light brown sugar
½ cup corn syrup
1 tablespoon butter or margarine

Preheat the slow cooker on HIGH.

Lightly grease a 8-cup ovenproof soufflé or similar dish. In a bowl, cream together ¼ cup of the butter or margarine with ⅓ cup of the sugar. Spread this mixture over base of prepared dish (see above). Set aside. In the same bowl, beat remaining butter or margarine and sugar together until creamy, then gradually beat in eggs. Fold in flour, then fold in dates and walnuts, and enough milk to make a soft, dropping consistency. Spoon this mixture into the dish and level the surface. Cover loosely with greased foil.

Stand the dish on top of a plain metal pastry cutter in the cooking pot of slow cooker. Add sufficient boiling water to come halfway up sides of dish. Cover and cook on HIGH for 3-4 hours or until a skewer inserted in center comes out clean. Place sauce ingredients in a small heavy pan. Heat gently, stirring, until the ingredients are melted; bring gently to a boil, stirring. Carefully invert pudding on to a warmed serving plate. Cut into wedges and serve with sauce poured over.

Serves 6-8

CRÈME CARAMEL

¾ cup superfine sugar
4 eggs
½ teaspoon vanilla extract
2½ cups milk

Preheat the slow cooker on HIGH. Grease an 7 inch soufflé dish or similar ovenproof dish and set aside. Put ½ cup of the sugar in a small pan with ⅔ cup of water. Heat gently, stirring, until sugar has dissolved, then bring to a boil and boil without stirring until the mixture caramelizes to a golden brown. Pour into the prepared dish and set aside.

Put the eggs, vanilla extract, and remaining sugar in a bowl and whisk together lightly. Set aside. Warm the milk in a saucepan, then pour on to egg mixture, whisking continuously. Strain over the cooled caramel. Cover the dish with foil, then place in the cooking pot of the slow cooker. Add sufficient boiling water to the cooking pot to come halfway up the sides of the dish.

Cover, reduce the temperature to LOW, and cook for 5-6 hours or until a knife inserted in the center comes out clean. Remove the dish from the slow cooker, uncover and leave to cool, then chill for several hours. Gently ease the dessert away from the sides of the dish and carefully turn out on to a serving plate. Serve with fresh fruit such as raspberries.

Serves 4-6

COOK'S TIP: Use half milk and half heavy cream in place of all milk, if preferred.

— FRUIT, NUT, & SPICE BREAD —

2 cups self-rising flour
1 teaspoon baking powder
2 teaspoons ground mixed spice
¾ cup light brown sugar
¾ cup golden raisins
¾ cup dark raisins
1 cup chopped ready-to-eat dried apricots
1 cup chopped mixed nuts such as hazelnuts and
   walnuts
2 eggs, beaten
⅔ cup milk

Preheat the slow cooker on HIGH. Lightly grease and line the bottom of a 2lb loaf tin and set aside.

Sift the flour, baking powder, and mixed spice into a bowl. Stir in the sugar, dried fruit, and nuts, mixing well. In a small bowl, beat the eggs and milk together, then add to the fruit mixture. Stir well until thoroughly mixed. Spoon the mixture into the prepared tin and level the surface. Cover loosely with greased foil. Stand the tin on top of a plain metal pastry cutter in the cooking pot of the slow cooker. Add sufficient boiling water to the cooking pot to come halfway up the sides of the tin.

Cover and cook on HIGH for 2-3 hours or until a skewer inserted in the center comes out clean. Lift the tin out of the slow cooker and leave to stand for 5 minutes. Turn the teabread out of the tin and leave to cool completely on a wire rack. Cut into slices to serve on its own or spread with butter.

Serves 8-10

VARAITIONS: Use chopped ready-to-eat dried pears in place of apricots. Use ground cinnamon or ginger in place of mixed spice.

—— BANANA & GINGER LOAF ——

½ cup butter (softened) or margarine
¾ cup light brown sugar
2 eggs, beaten
2 cups self-rising white flour
pinch of salt
2 teaspoons ground ginger
2 large bananas
a little lemon juice
3 pieces preserved stem ginger, drained and finely
  chopped (optional)

Preheat the slow cooker on HIGH. Lightly grease and line a 2lb loaf tin and set aside.

In a bowl, beat together the butter or margarine and sugar until pale and fluffy. Gradually beat in eggs, then fold in flour, salt, and ground ginger. Peel and mash bananas with a little lemon juice, then fold them into the mixture until well combined. Fold in stem ginger, if using. Spoon mixture into the prepared tin and level surface. Cover loosely with greased foil. Stand tin on top of a plain metal pastry cutter in the cooking pot of the slow cooker. Add sufficient boiling water to the cooking pot to come halfway up the sides of the tin.

Cover and cook on HIGH for 2-3 hours or until a skewer inserted in the center of the loaf comes out clean. Lift the tin out of the slow cooker and leave to stand for 5 minutes. Turn the loaf out of the tin and leave to cool on a wire rack. Cut into slices to serve.

Serves 8-10

VARIATIONS: Use ground mixed spice, cinnamon, or nutmeg in place of ginger.

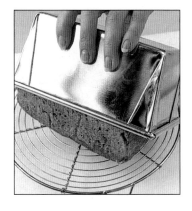

RICH CHOCOLATE CAKE

FOR THE CAKE:
¾ cup butter (softened) or margarine
½ cup light brown sugar
¼ cup honey
3 eggs, beaten
1 cup self-rising flour
pinch of salt
6 tablespoons cocoa powder
1 teaspoon instant coffee in 1 tablespoon hot water
½ teaspoon vanilla extract
FOR THE FROSTING:
7oz plain chocolate, broken into squares
½ cup butter or margarine
1¼ cups confectioners' sugar, sifted
4 tablespoons light cream
chocolate curls, to decorate

Preheat slow cooker on HIGH. Grease and line an 7 inch round cake tin. In a bowl, cream together butter, sugar, and honey until fluffy (see above). Gradually beat in eggs. Sift in flour, salt, and cocoa powder; fold into mixture with dissolved coffee and vanilla until well mixed. Spoon into prepared tin and level surface. Cover loosely with greased foil. Stand tin on top of a plain metal pastry cutter in cooking pot of slow cooker. Add boiling water to come halfway up sides of tin. Cover and cook on HIGH for 2-3 hours or until a skewer inserted in center comes out clean.

Lift tin out and leave to stand for 5 minutes. Turn cake out and cool completely on a wire rack. For the frosting, melt chocolate and butter in a bowl set over a pan of simmering water, stirring. Remove from heat, add sugar and cream and beat until smooth and thickened slightly. Cool, then cover and chill until frosting holds its shape. Cut cake in half horizontally; sandwich together with one-third of frosting. Spread remaining frosting over top and sides. Decorate with chocolate curls.

Serves 8-10

—— CARROT & ORANGE CAKE ——

¾ cup butter (softened) or margarine
1 cup light brown sugar
finely grated zest of 1 orange
3 eggs, beaten
1½ cups self-rising flour, sifted
1 teaspoon ground cinnamon
1 cup finely grated peeled carrots
1 cup full fat soft cheese
2 teaspoons honey
1 teaspoon orange juice
chopped walnuts, to decorate

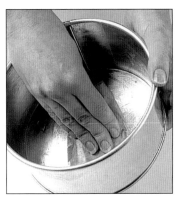

Preheat the slow cooker on HIGH. Lightly grease and line an 7 inch round cake tin; set aside.

In a bowl, cream butter or margarine and sugar together until pale and fluffy. Reserve ½ teaspoon orange zest for topping and stir remaining orange zest into the creamed mixture. Gradually beat in eggs. Fold in flour and cinnamon, then fold in carrots, mixing well. Turn mixture into prepared tin and level the surface. Cover loosely with greased foil. Stand the tin on top of a plain metal pastry cutter in cooking pot of slow cooker. Add sufficient boiling water to cooking pot to come halfway up sides of tin.

Cover and cook on HIGH for 3-5 hours or until a skewer inserted in the center of the cake comes out clean. Lift the tin out of the slow cooker and leave to stand for 5 minutes. Turn the cake out of the tin and leave to cool completely on a wire rack. To make the topping, in a bowl, beat together the cream cheese, honey, orange juice, and reserved orange zest until well mixed. Spread over the top of the cooled cake and sprinkle with chopped walnuts to decorate. Serve in slices.

Serves 8-10

CINNAMON-SPICED APPLE CAKE

½ cup butter (softened) or margarine
¾ cup light brown sugar
2 eggs, beaten
2 cups self-rising white flour
½ teaspoon baking powder
1½ teaspoons ground cinnamon
1½ cups chopped cooking apples
½ cup golden raisins
3-4 tablespoons milk
2 tablespoons brown granulated sugar (optional)

Preheat the slow cooker on HIGH while preparing the cake mixture.

Lightly grease and line an 7 inch round deep cake tin and set aside (see above). In a bowl, cream the butter or margarine and sugar together until pale and fluffy. Gradually beat in the eggs. Mix the flours, baking powder, and cinnamon together, then fold into creamed mixture. Fold in apples, golden raisins, and enough milk to give a soft, dropping consistency. Turn the mixture into the prepared tin and level surface. Cover loosely with greased foil. Stand the tin on top of a plain metal pastry cutter in the cooking pot of the slow cooker.

Add sufficient boiling water to come halfway up the sides of the tin. Cover and cook on HIGH for 3-5 hours or until a skewer inserted in center of the cake comes out clean. Lift the tin out of the slow cooker and leave to stand for 5 minutes. Turn the cake out and leave to cool on a wire rack. If you like, brush the top of hot cake with a little water, then sprinkle brown granulated sugar over the top. Serve warm or cold in slices. Serve on its own or with custard, cream, or ice cream.

Serves 8-10

PINEAPPLE UPSIDE-DOWN CAKE

6 tablespoons corn or maple syrup
8oz can pineapple rings in fruit juice, drained
9 small ready-to-eat dried apricots
½ cup butter (softened) or margarine
¾ cup light brown sugar
2 eggs, beaten
1½ cups self-rising flour, sifted
2 tablespoons cocoa powder, sifted
3-4 tablespoons milk

Preheat the slow cooker on HIGH while preparing the mixture. Lightly grease and line the bottom of a 7 inch round ovenproof soufflé dish or deep cake tin and set aside.

Spoon the syrup evenly over the base of prepared dish or tin. Arrange the pineapple rings and apricots in the syrup. Set aside. In a bowl, cream butter or margarine and sugar together until pale and fluffy. Gradually beat in eggs. Fold in flour and cocoa powder, adding enough milk to make a soft, dropping consistency. Spread the mixture evenly over the fruit and level the surface. Cover loosely with greased foil. Stand the dish or tin on top of a plain metal pastry cutter in the cooking pot of the slow cooker.

Add sufficient boiling water to the cooking pot to come halfway up the sides of the dish or tin. Cover and cook on HIGH for 3-4 hours or until a skewer inserted in the center of the cake comes out clean. Lift the tin or dish out of the slow cooker and leave to stand for 5 minutes. Invert the cake on to a serving plate and serve warm or cold in wedges. Serve on its own or with heavy cream, custard, or ice cream.

Serves 6-8

GINGERBREAD

2 cups all-purpose flour
pinch of salt
1 teaspoon baking powder
2 teaspoons ground ginger
½ teaspoon ground mixed spice
½ teaspoon baking soda
6 tablespoons butter or margarine
¾ cup light brown sugar
½ cup corn syrup
⅔ cup milk
1 egg, beaten

Preheat the slow cooker on HIGH. Lightly grease and line an 7 inch round deep cake tin or a 2lb loaf tin and set aside.

Sift flour, salt, baking powder, ginger, mixed spice, and baking soda into a bowl and stir to mix. Place butter or margarine, sugar, and syrup in a saucepan and heat gently until melted and blended, stirring occasionally. Remove the pan from the heat and cool slightly. Make a well in the center of the dry ingredients, pour in syrup mixture, add milk and egg, and beat together until smooth and thoroughly mixed. Pour into the prepared tin and cover loosely with greased foil.

Stand the tin on top of a plain metal pastry cutter in the cooking pot of the slow cooker. Add sufficient boiling water to come halfway up the sides of the tin. Cover and cook on HIGH for 4-7 hours or until a skewer inserted in the center comes out clean. Lift the tin out of slow cooker and leave to stand for 5 minutes. Turn gingerbread out and leave to cool on a wire rack. Cut into slices to serve. Serve warm or cold on its own or with custard.

Serves 8-10

— SWEET MANGO CHUTNEY —

3lb firm, ripe mangoes (about 3 large mangoes)
8oz cooking apples
8oz onions
2 cloves garlic, crushed
2 cups chopped ready-to-eat dried apricots
2 cups light brown sugar
2 teaspoons ground ginger
1 teaspoon ground cinnamon
½ teaspoon salt
⅔ cup cider vinegar

Preheat the slow cooker on HIGH while preparing the ingredients. Peel and remove the seeds of the mangoes, then chop.

Peel, core, and chop the apples and skin and finely chop the onions. Place mangoes, apples, onions, garlic, apricots, sugar, spices, salt, and vinegar in a pan and heat gently, stirring, until the sugar has dissolved.

Bring to a boil, then transfer to the cooking pot. Cover and cook on HIGH for 7-9 hours (or cook on LOW for 10-12 hours), or until the chutney is soft and thickened, stirring occasionally during cooking, if possible. Stir well, then spoon the chutney into warm, sterilized jars, cover, cool, seal, and label. Process in a hot-water bath if desired. Store in a cool, dry, dark place and allow to mature for 2-3 months before using.

Makes about 5lb

RED TOMATO CHUTNEY

3lb tomatoes, peeled
1lb cooking apples
2 onions
3 cloves garlic, crushed
1 cup raisins
1½ cups light brown sugar
2 teaspoons ground ginger
1 teaspoon ground nutmeg
1 teaspoon ground coriander
1 teaspoon ground cumin
⅔ cup red wine vinegar

Preheat the slow cooker on HIGH while preparing the ingredients.

Roughly chop the tomatoes, peel, core, and dice the apples, and skin and finely chop the onions. Place the tomatoes, apples, onions, garlic, raisins, sugar, spices, and vinegar in a pan and heat gently, stirring, until the sugar has dissolved. Bring to a boil, then transfer to the cooking pot. Cover and cook on HIGH for 8-10 hours (or cook on LOW for 10-14 hours), or until the chutney is soft and thickened, stirring occasionally during cooking, if possible.

Stir well, then spoon the chutney into warm, sterilized jars, cover, cool, seal, and label. Process in a hot-water bath if desired. Store in a cool, dry, dark place and allow to mature for 2-3 months before using.

Makes about 5lb

APPLE & RAISIN CHUTNEY

3lb cooking apples
2lb onions
2 cups golden raisins
1½lb light brown sugar
2 teaspoons salt
3 teaspoons ground mixed spice
1 teaspoon cayenne pepper
scant 1 cup malt vinegar

Preheat the slow cooker on HIGH while preparing the ingredients. Peel, core, and dice the apples, and skin and finely chop the onions.

Place the apples, onions, golden raisins, sugar, salt, mixed spice, cayenne pepper, and vinegar in a large pan and mix well. Heat gently, stirring, until the sugar has dissolved, then bring to a boil. Transfer to the cooking pot. Cover and cook on HIGH for 6-8 hours (or cook on LOW for 10-12 hours), or until the chutney is soft and thickened, stirring occasionally during cooking, if possible.

Stir well, then spoon the chutney into warm sterilized jars, cover, cool, seal, and label. Process in a hot-water bath if desired. Store in a cool, dry, dark place and allow to mature for 2-3 months before using.

Makes about 5lb

FRESH ORANGE CURD

½ cup unsalted butter
finely grated zest and juice of 2 oranges
finely grated zest and juice of 1 lemon
1½ cups superfine sugar
4 eggs, lightly beaten

Place the butter, orange and lemon zests and juices, and sugar in a saucepan and heat gently, stirring, until the butter has melted, the sugar has dissolved, and the ingredients are blended together.

Remove the pan from the heat, pour the mixture into a 5 cup pudding basin, and leave to cool. Preheat the slow cooker on HIGH for 10-15 minutes. Whisk the eggs into the cooled mixture.

Cover the basin with foil and stand it in the cooking pot of the slow cooker. Add sufficient boiling water to the cooking pot to come halfway up the sides of the basin. Cover, reduce the temperature to LOW, and cook for 3-4 hours, or until thickened, stirring occasionally during cooking, if possible. Stir well, then pour into warm, sterilized jars, cool, seal, and label. Store in the refrigerator and use within 3-4 weeks.

Makes about 2¼lb

LEMON & LIME CURD

½ cup unsalted butter
finely grated zest and juice of 2 lemons
finely grated zest and juice of 2 limes
1lb superfine sugar
4 eggs, lightly beaten

Place the butter, lemon and lime zests and juices, and sugar in a saucepan and heat gently, stirring, until the butter has melted, the sugar has dissolved, and the ingredients are blended together.

Remove the pan from the heat, pour the mixture into a 5 cup pudding basin, and leave to cool. Preheat the slow cooker on HIGH for 10-15 minutes. Whisk the eggs into the cooled mixture.

Cover the basin with foil and stand it in the cooking pot of the slow cooker. Add sufficient boiling water to the cooking pot to come halfway up the sides of the basin. Cover, reduce the temperature to LOW, and cook for 3-4 hours, or until thickened, stirring occasionally during cooking, if possible. Stir well, then pour into warm, sterilized jars, cool, seal, and label. Store in the refrigerator and use within 3-4 weeks.

Makes about 2¼lb

MULLED WINE

½ cup superfine sugar
1 bottle (750ml) red wine such as Burgundy or
  Bordeaux
2 cinnamon sticks
4-6 whole cloves
2 oranges, thinly sliced
1 lemon, thinly sliced

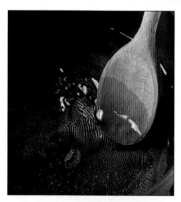

Preheat the slow cooker on HIGH while preparing the mulled wine. Place the sugar in a pan with 2 cups water. Heat gently, stirring, until the sugar has dissolved, then bring to a boil.

Remove the pan from the heat and stir in the wine and spices. Pour into the cooking pot, cover, reduce the temperature to LOW, and cook for 4-6 hours or until the mulled wine is hot.

Remove and discard the spices, stir in the orange and lemon slices, and serve hot in warm glasses.

Makes about 5 cups. Serves 8-10

COOK'S TIP: Use a ready-prepared sachet of mulled wine spice in place of adding the spices above. Simply add the sachet to the sugar liquid with the wine.

RUM & BRANDY TODDY

2 lemons
1 cup sugar
2⅓ cups rum
2⅓ cups brandy
1 teaspoon ground nutmeg
1 teaspoon ground cinnamon

Preheat the slow cooker on HIGH while preparing the toddy. Squeeze the juice from the lemons and strain into a saucepan.

Add the sugar and 5 cups of water and heat gently, stirring, until the sugar has dissolved. Remove the pan from the heat and stir in the rum, brandy, and ground spices.

Pour into the cooking pot, cover, reduce the temperature to LOW, and cook for 4-6 hours or until hot. Serve hot in warm glasses.

Makes about 9 cups. Serves 12-15

SPICED FRUIT PUNCH

⅓ cup light brown sugar
4½ cups unsweetened orange juice
4½ cups unsweetened apple juice
1 teaspoon ground ginger
1 teaspoon ground mixed spice
2 whole cloves
1 cinnamon stick
1-2 eating apples, thinly sliced
1 orange, thinly sliced

Preheat the slow cooker on HIGH while preparing the punch. Place the sugar in a pan with 1¼ cups of water. Heat gently, stirring, until the sugar has dissolved.

Pour into the cooking pot, then stir in the fruit juices and ground and whole spices. Cover, reduce the temperature to LOW, and cook for 4-6 hours or until the punch is hot.

Remove and discard the whole spices, stir in the apple and orange slices, and serve hot in warm glasses.

Makes about 10 cups. Serves 12-16

— SPICED CRANBERRY PUNCH —

4½ cups unsweetened cranberry juice
⅓ cup light brown sugar
scant 1 cup unsweetened orange juice
2 cinnamon sticks
4 whole cloves
4 cardamom pods, bruised
2 oranges, thinly sliced

Preheat the slow cooker on HIGH for 15-20 minutes. Meanwhile, pour the cranberry juice into a saucepan, add the sugar, and heat gently, stirring, until the sugar dissolves.

Remove the pan from the heat and stir in the orange juice and spices. Transfer to the cooking pot, cover, reduce the temperature to LOW, and cook for 4-6 hours or until hot.

Strain into a warm pitcher, stir in the orange slices, and serve hot in warm glasses.

Makes about 5 cups. Serves 6-8

VARIATION: Use still cider in place of cranberry juice for a hot spiced cider punch.

INDEX

Apple and raisin chutney 89
Apricot bread pudding 70
Bacon and corn chowder 12
Banana and ginger loaf 81
Barbecue baked beans 66
Barbecue chicken 45
Beef goulash with chili 26
Beef in red wine 28
Braised duck with orange 54
Braised pork with cabbage 34
Carrot and orange cake 83
Cheese fondue 22
Cheesy zucchini strata 61
Chicken and chickpea stew 43
Chicken liver pâté 24
Chicken tagine with figs 50
Chicken with shallots 44
Chili con carne 30
Chocolate fondue 69
Cinnamon baked apples 77
Cinnamon-spiced apple cake 84
Coq au vin 42
Country chicken casserole 47
Creamy lemon rice dessert 76
Creamy watercress soup 16
Crème caramel 79
Curried pot roast beef 29
Curried turkey with coconut 53
Date and walnut pudding 78
Eggplant dip 25
Farmhouse pâté 23

Festive plum pudding 73
Fragrant chicken curry 46
Fresh lemon sponge pudding 72
Fresh mushroom soup 18
Fresh orange curd 90
Fruit and nut pilaf 65
Fruit, nut, and spice bread 80
Garden vegetable soup 17
Gingerbread 86
Harvest vegetable hotpot 63
Honey and mustard glazed ham 39
Italian chicken cassoulet 48
Lamb and apricot tagine 31
Lamb and bell pepper hotpot 33
Leek and potato soup 14
Lemon and lime curd 91
Lemon-baked chicken 49
Macaroni and broccoli bake 58
Mediterranean vegetable stew 67
Mexican bean soup 21
Mulled wine 92
Pea and ham soup 13
Pineapple upside-down cake 85
Plum tomato and basil soup 15
Pork and bean cassoulet 35
Poussin braised in wine 51
Ratatouille beanpot 57

Red tomato chutney 88
Rhubarb with orange and ginger 71
Rice pudding with orange 75
Rich chocolate cake 82
Root vegetable casserole 59
Root vegetable curry 64
Rum and brandy toddy 93
Salmon and broccoli risotto 41
Sausage and leek casserole 38
Sausage and mushroom hotpot 37
Spiced cranberry punch 95
Spiced fruit punch 94
Spicy squash soup 19
Stewed lamb with rosemary 32
Stuffed bell peppers 56
Sweet and sour meatballs 36
Sweet mango chutney 87
Tasty beef and bean stew 27
Thai spiced chicken soup 20
Tipsy pears 74
Tuna and tomato casserole 40
Turkey and mushroom risotto 52
Vegetable chili bake 60
Vegetable ragoût 62
Venison casserole 55
Winter fruit compote 68